The Ark II

The End

by Ian C. Jervis

ISBN: 9781978347632

Dedication

To my Lisa, who is not only the love of my life, but is my life. She is my inspiration and my reason why. She is also in real term a co-author of this book, full of creativity and ideas. Thank you, Lisa, I love you.

To Yahweh, the Most High Elohim, the Maker of All things and the very reason that I breathe. I pray that by reading this that people are drawn to you, find you and love you for themselves in the way that I love you.

CONTENTS

Introduction

Those who have read 'The Ark' will know that 'The Ark II has been four years in the making. So, first of all, thank you for being patient! The idea for the book was already there after 'The Ark', however, the way it needed to be delivered and the content it needed to contain evolved during the process of writing the book.

In keeping with the prequel, although this is a fictional story, the content is based on our own journey of refinement and learning in our walk with our King, Yahshua (Jesus). I say 'we' because my wife, Lisa, has been very involved in the creating of this novel and this work would not have been possible without her input.

If you haven't read 'The Ark' part one, please do so because elements of part two will not make a great deal of sense without part one.

I truly hope that these books are a sincere blessing in your lives and inspire you to walk ever closer to Yahweh through the grace of Yahshua.

Blessings,

Ian.

Chapter One

The End

Lisa opened her eyes and shook her head. Everything was dark. She couldn't see a thing, not even her hand in front of her face. A feeling of panic began building up inside of her which increased as she heard the sound of children screaming and had no idea where Luke and Josh were. She felt her stomach pounding as fear tried to grip and envelop her. An air of fear was building quickly as people began crying and shouting when they realised that they couldn't see.

"Luke, Josh!" Lisa shouted but heard no response from them. She got up onto her hands and knees and started groping around trying to feel for something; anything that would give her a clue as to where she was in relation to her surroundings. All she could feel was feathery grass beneath her hands. She felt lost and completely disorientated.

She sat upright, trying to look for a 'chink' of light in the black mass in front of her, desperately searching for a glimmer, but there was nothing.

The great flash from the heavens had caused a blindness that had left her and everyone around her, in the dark; confused and bewildered. In the blink of an eye they had gone from being highly elated, in the company of Yahshua, their Saviour, to being in complete darkness and feeling afraid.

Lisa sat for a moment trying to calm herself and gather her thoughts. She knew that despite her own bewilderment Yahweh was watching over them all and they would be okay. She knew that she had to do something to try to calm and reassure other people. One thing she had learned was that where there was confusion and panic; there the devil would be also. She shouted,

"Stay calm everyone, we will be okay!" but nobody could hear her because of the pandemonium all around, apart from a few people around her.

"Lisa!" came a cry from a voice she immediately recognised which gave her an instant warm, secure feeling, "Where are you?" She scrambled on all fours in the direction of that voice she knew and loved and with her outstretched arm she touched a hand which was also reaching out for her.

"Charles!" she cried, full of tears. He replied in the same manner,

"Lisa, sweetheart!" They squeezed each other tightly.

"Oh Charles!" she asked, "Are you okay? Where are the boys?"

"I'm fine," replied Charles, "and I think I heard the boys a moment ago, I just can't see anything!

Lisa continued, "Me neither and I assume everyone else is the same, but I think this will only be temporary. We'll be fine, we need to calm everybody down and find our boys!" Lisa let go of Charles' grip on her and felt for his hand, so as not to lose him again and shouted at the top of her voice for everyone to calm down. Her little voice hardly impacted the furore that was going on all around them. Charles joined in with her and little by little a calmness descended on the crowd.

"Everybody, listen! It's me, Lisa!" her voice was a little hoarse with all the shouting. She continued, "Don't be afraid! Remember what Yahshua said to us all just a short while ago; we will have to go through many trials during this time and this is just the first! It's just a test! Now let's be strong and get through this together! Let's not fall at the first small hurdle, we may have many more to come, but we will be okay! He is here with us all!" Just then somebody shouted,

"I can see something! My eyes! They are starting to clear!" Then another,

"Me too! I can see light!"

People cheered as more and more eyes were opened. Shouts of 'HalleluYah' could be heard all around the meadow, echoing across the valley. Lisa began again,

"You see!" she shouted, "Yahweh is awesome! He will take care of us!" People cheered with grateful hearts. She continued,

"And if any of you that can see, spot my boys, can you please bring them over to me!"

Lisa sat down with Charles, holding each other's hands.

"Can you see anything, yet Charles?" she asked.

"Nothing!" He replied, "but I'm okay, at least I have hold of you." Lisa squeezed his hand and leant on his strong shoulder as they sat there on the grass, waiting for their eyes to recover.

"Hey guys!" came another familiar voice, "Are you still in the dark?" It was Sam, joking as usual. He still had slightly blurred vision but could see enough to be able to make out Charles and Lisa sitting down on the grass.

"Sam!" they both exclaimed, "Yes we are I'm afraid."

3

"I have your two princes here, Lisa." Sam replied.

"Mummy!!" cried the boys in unison, desperate for the arms of their mother,

"Luke! Josh!" Lisa squealed with joy and hugged them both. The boys could both see now but Sophie, who had been with them through the whole ordeal was still blind and so Luke and Josh had hold of her hands, guiding her for a change.

"Are you okay, Sophie?" asked Lisa,

"Yes, I'm fine Lisa," replied Sophie who seemed a little taken aback, "I just hope this doesn't last too long!"

"Me too, Sophie" Lisa agreed.

"How is everyone else, Sam?" asked Charles.

"Everybody seems fine!" said Sam, "Just a little shook up by the whole experience. It will be good to get back to the house and try to get things back to normal." Lisa agreed and held out her hand for Sam to lift her up while Charles clumsily scrambled up onto his feet. Sam then linked his arms through theirs and began to slowly walk with them through the throngs of people sat on the grass.

He guided them across the meadow and down the hill towards the house. Others began to follow them; those that could see, helped those that couldn't which caused a lot of laughter and jollity, which was so good to hear; an eternity away from the screams of panic and terror they had been witnessing a few minutes earlier. On the way down, Sam whispered to Lisa and Charles,

"You should see the sky, guys!"

"What's wrong with it?" asked Lisa in a concerned tone of voice.

"Well it's hard to describe!" said Sam, "I can't see perfectly yet, but the Sun and Moon seem to be sitting side by side and there is a huge glow directly above us! It looks very weird!"

"It sounds just like the vision I had, Sam," said Lisa, "The flash was the three stars in the belt of Orion exploding. It will be as bright as another Sun."

"Oh, it is Lisa, it is!" replied Sam emphatically.

He slowly guided them down the path from the meadow toward the yard. As they went, they could hear cries of joy coming from behind them as more and more people began to regain their sight. Lisa explained to the boys what had happened and that soon Mummy, and Charles would be able to see too and that they needed to give Yahweh thanks for taking care of them all and keeping them safe. In no time at all the boys were running around, re-enacting the whole episode in their own cute way.

It seemed to take forever to wind their way down the hill to the house; every step had to be trodden carefully as even the guide himself couldn't see as well as he normally could, although he was improving with every passing minute. They ventured around the corner of a group of trees, to within sight of the house, when Sam suddenly stopped in his tracks.

"No way!" he cried, "Surely not!"

"What is it Sam? What's the matter?" asked Lisa, concerned by the desperation in Sam's voice.

"I can't see one hundred percent, Lisa" Sam continued, almost in tears, "but if my eyes aren't deceiving me, the old house has been completely flattened!"

"What?!" cried Charles.

"No!" echoed Lisa, "Our beautiful home! How can it be?"

They hurried down the path as fast as they dare go in their condition, desperate to know for certain. They came onto the yard and Sam confirmed what he had seen. Lisa wept bitterly.

"Why!?" she cried and looked up towards the heavens, "I don't understand!"

"It's worse than I thought!" said Sam in a despairing voice, "All the buildings are down too!"

They wandered around the wreckages in the farmyard; Sam describing the desolation that surrounded them.

"Tell me we still have the bunkhouses?" exclaimed Lisa.

"I'm not sure! I can't see them yet!" replied Sam leading them slowly, shuffling across the yard so he could take a look.

"I can't believe what I'm looking at!" exclaimed Sam, "They are all down, Lisa! Every single one of them!"

They stood there in the middle of the yard dumbfounded. People gathered around, saddened and confused; looking at Lisa and Charles for some inspiration. She tried to console those around her, but she really didn't know what to say to them because she had no idea herself. This was supposed to be their refuge and safe place. Now it was gone, and she didn't know what to do. She hung her head and prayed to Yahweh for help, remembering what Yahshua had said to them before the flash; that they should be strong and that He would be with them always.

"Be with me now, my Saviour." She muttered to herself and lifted her head to speak words which she hoped would reassure the crowd.

"I hope you can all hear me okay." she said, with a hoarse almost broken voice. "It seems that everything has been flattened by the earthquake, so we have an immediate situation on our hands. We need to pull together as quickly as we can and build some sort of shelters to get us all through the night." An eerie silence filled the place. "Maybe everyone who can see, even if partially, could go with Sam and find anything that can be used to make shelters. Please stay strong and remember that God is with us and we will come through this! He knew this was going to happen and He will protect us. It may be uncomfortable right now, but we will survive."

Suddenly Charles jumped up and shouted,

"HalleluYah!! Let there be light!" His sight was finally beginning to return. He kissed Lisa on the cheek and wobbled down the yard with Sam and those with some vision. There must have been a hundred or so people who could now see to some extent.

Lisa sat down right where she stood in the middle of the yard along with the rest of the blind. She held her head in her hands. She whispered to herself and her Father,

"Why has all this happened when we have all worked so hard?" She sighed and tried to muster all her inner strength as she sat there on the floor in complete darkness with people wandering about all around her.

"I'm with you, Lisa!" cried a voice she recognised very well. It was Jenny.

"Jenny!" Lisa answered tearfully, scrambling to her feet, pleased to hear her friends familiar voice. She dug up a smile and reached out in the direction of her voice to give her a hug. They sobbed together as they embraced. Lisa asked tearfully,

"Oh Jenny! How's Ben?"

"He's fine! He's working with the others!" Jenny replied trying not to cry.

"Oh, that's good!" said a slightly subdued Lisa, "Have you seen Jim and Connie?"

"We're here too, Lisa!" came Jim's dulcet tone. Lisa smiled and held open her arms to hug them both. It felt great to hold them in her arms. The family was still all together. They all sat back down on the ground. Despite her own feelings, Lisa knew she had to do her part to keep spirits high.

"So, is everyone here happy?!" Lisa enquired of those around her and received back a unanimous positive affirmation.

"Good, good!" she said with a smile, finding herself comforted by the strength and faith of her friends, new and old.

As they all chatted together, sat there on the grass in the middle of the yard, people would randomly jump up as their sight came back; usually with a "Praise God!" or "HalleluYah!" The newly sighted then wandered off and joined the rest making shelters, fires and preparing what food that they could find. One thing was for certain, was that the food they had stored would not last the crowd that they now had up there on the mountain, for very long at all. They knew, however, that Father God would take care of them all and not let them suffer. They had no home, no electricity and no idea what to do in this situation, but they did have faith and the power of mighty Yahweh.

One by one people regained their sight and got up and went to work, leaving Lisa telling stories about the incredible happenings of the last year and how their relationship with the Father, had totally changed their lives. Jenny, Jim and Connie all recovered but still Lisa could not see a thing and as she sat with an ever-diminishing crowd, she wondered to herself if she was going to be the last one to regain her sight. Just as the thought passed through her head, the last few people around her suddenly all stood up together with shouts of, "I can see!" and "Praise God!" Sight had returned to them all; all except Lisa. They ran off, jumping for joy, to find their loved ones and to help everyone else, leaving Lisa sat all alone in the middle of the yard.

She pondered on God's words that Isaiah wrote when He said, 'Fear not for I am with you! Do not be dismayed for I am your God and I will strengthen you....'

"....and I will help you!" she shouted out, "and uphold you with my righteous right hand!" She knew Yahweh was speaking to her. Again, she cried out,

"Faith without works is dead!" A few 'Amens' came from those busily working away around her. She suddenly felt the urge to stand up and walk, so she got to her feet and tentatively took a step, in complete darkness, not really having a clue where she was other than in the yard somewhere. As she did, the strangest thing began to happen; a picture appeared in front of her, in her mind's eye, showing her exactly where she was. It was almost like her own personal satellite navigation system. She took more steps. Suddenly someone crossed her path right in front of her, not knowing that she couldn't see. Lisa stopped abruptly without any collision.

"Wow! Father You are amazing! Yahweh you are awesome!" she exclaimed,

"What can you not do?!"

There was no reply; which was answer enough. She wandered around, feeling like she was almost in another realm, walking in the spirit. The more she walked the easier it became; she could see in her mind's eye obstacles nearby.

"Lisa! What are you doing?!" came a familiar, concerned voice. It was Charles. "Can you see?!"

"Not yet!" exclaimed Lisa, Charles shook his head and tried to take her arm,

"Why are you walking about on your own then? Let me   walk with you?" he insisted.

"No, I'm fine!" Lisa replied emphatically, pushing his hand away, "I need to do this! Yahweh is teaching; helping me to hear better!"

"Well, be careful won't you!" laughed Charles wanting to take care of his wife but knowing that she'd do whatever she thought God was telling her to do anyway. Lisa smiled. It was lovely to have someone care for her in that way; something she'd never experienced before in her life. She replied,

"Thank you, Charles but I'm in good hands!" Charles knew exactly what she meant, which was good enough for him. He said,

"Everyone else can see now, apart from you, but to be honest, Lisa, there isn't a great deal to look at anyway! There's not much that we can salvage from all the wreckage, the buildings have been completely destroyed! People are collecting their personal belongings and that's about all they can do. We have an upturned silo that we can shelter in from any rain, but as for anywhere for people to stay we are going to have to completely rebuild from scratch!"

"Goodness me! All that work!" Lisa replied, saddened at the thought of starting again, "But if we can just make do for tonight, I know God has a plan! Yahweh is faithful!"

Charles lowered his voice, looking around himself as he did and said,

"Lisa, I have to tell you. Sam said he heard some people

talking about heading back down to Hightown!" Lisa sighed and shook her head, slightly dismayed.

"No, we need to stick together!" she said. "Let's make a fire and gather everyone around. They'll find it so much worse down there! Can you organise it?"

"Yes of course!" Charles replied, "I'll do it right now!"

"Thank you." responded Lisa "You are so good!" Charles smiled and wandered off to find Sam. Lisa shouted to him as he walked away,

"Charles! Is there anything left of the house?"

"Oh no, it's a write-off!" he laughed regretfully, "I'll rescue what I can of our things in the morning! Come on, walk with me and I'll get things organised!"

"No, you go, Charles!" Lisa replied, "I need to practise!" Charles laughed and went off to gather everyone together.

She whispered to God,

"Why has this all happened? Wasn't this supposed to be a place of refuge, where people could hide away from the troubles? How is this going to work now?"

"The Ark isn't the house, Lisa!" a soft voice said in her head, "Or the buildings!"

"Oh!" she cried, slightly taken aback by His answer. Immediately the words from the book of Jeremiah came to her mind,

"Stand at the crossroads and look! Ask for the ancient path! Ask where the good way is and walk in it. There you will find rest for your souls!"

Lisa pondered for a while; knowing the scripture but not understanding how it applied to their situation; this dilemma they found themselves in. She cried out,

"So, what is the Ark?"

Chapter Two

The Crossroads

Lisa cautiously walked down to the area where the buildings used to stand, using her God given 'vision' to navigate obstacles and listening intently to her surroundings. She could hear the voices of people muttering to one another, coming to her from what seemed like every direction. They were complaining about their circumstances; some saying that it was going to be cold in the night and others saying that maybe they should go back to their houses in Hightown. She could also hear others trying to lift their spirits and encourage them, but this was causing disagreements and friction. The voices kept coming at her from all around, bombarding her, one after another making her head spin and feel deeply uncomfortable. She could feel fear and anxiety rising again as she could hear peoples concerns and questions as though they were being were thrown at her personally.

"What is happening with the Sun and Moon?! This can't be right!" said one.

Another said "What if there is another explosion?! What if more stars explode?! What are we going to do then?!" And yet another voice, which felt right by her side whispered to her,

"What if something worse happens?! People are scared!

We need to figure something out quickly!"

She began to feel completely overwhelmed and out of her depth and her mind took her back to her past when she had been so deeply wounded by the criticism of others. She remembered how she had felt so useless; as a child, as a teenager growing up and as a wife and mother before she had the encounter with God that changed her life. Just as she was on the brink of being consumed by panic, she suddenly recalled those precious words, 'You are far more powerful than you have been led to believe!' She remembered how Father God had grabbed hold of her, wrapped His big arms around her and changed her life in an incredible way. This was an opportunity to show that same love to His precious children, who right now had been thrown into the unknown. She knew this was what God needed her to do for these people who were tired and very scared after all they had been though; seeing their world turned upside down.

She walked on across the yard in the direction of voices. Some were laughing and chattering, still more were grumbling and arguing. The sound of wood crackling, the smell of burning and the warmth in the air told her she was near to the fire and by the familiar voices she could hear she knew she was at the meeting place. Charles rushed over to help her.

"I'm okay, really Charles!" she said, laughing. "I'm getting quite used to this!"

Everybody gathered around the fire and sat down, giving Lisa the opportunity to say a few words to them all. She sent a little prayer out to Yahweh in her head,

"Help me with the words, Father." She heard that still small voice inside her say,

"Compassion, they just need compassion, Lisa!
.... Just love them!"

She sat down among them and smiled, the words of her Father reverberating around in her head,

14

"Hi everyone!" Most echoed in reply. She continued,

"I know it has been an incredible day; one like we've never witnessed before. Just hours ago, we were all with our Saviour Yahshua, celebrating and enjoying a great feast and now it seems that we need saving again! I don't have a plan for this, I don't have answers. But I do know that we serve a mighty God. He knows exactly what we need to do. But He wants us to trust Him right now and do the best we can with what we have. The signs in the sky are a warning for us of the impending trouble; Now more than ever we need to put our faith into action and not let fear override. We all have to prepare our hearts and souls for Yahshua's return. Our faith is shown through our actions and the words we speak so as I said earlier, let's not fall or fail at this hurdle, or through any of the challenges to come."

Words just seemed to flow from her mouth and faith began to stir in the heart of the people as she spoke.

"If we can just get through tonight, everything will look different tomorrow, trust me! No, don't trust me, trust God!" She looked around at the faces before her and although she couldn't physically see them, she could feel their worries and uncertainties. You have been brought here to this place called the Ark which is a refuge for you and I know it doesn't look much like one now, but I know that we will all see things change very soon. Things are a lot worse down there in Hightown than they are here but if you do feel you have to leave, I do understand. But for those who are willing to stay and work through this together let's carry on and salvage whatever we can from all of the remains of the buildings. At least we have plenty of wood for the fire and we are all physically well, Praise Yahweh!" Everyone nodded in agreement.

"Yahweh will take good care of us! I know He will! He loves us! Let's love Him back by fully trusting Him and praising Him through all things."

Her words touched the people and were exactly what they all needed to hear. Peace and unity returned once more to the Ark along with a sense of relief and a confidence that things were going to turn out alright.

People began 'buzzing' around building make-shift shelters to sleep in and rescuing what they could from the ruins; pulling anything from the wreckage that could be useful in the days ahead. Charles, Lisa and the boys decided to sleep at the back of the farmhouse where there was a small group of trees. It was a nice spot, relatively sheltered and they could still feel the heat from the fire, floating on the night breeze.

Jim and Connie had volunteered their R.V. for shelter and had attracted quite a crowd. Even though two wheels had fallen into a large crack in the hard standing making it lean over quite severely, it was definitely the most comfortable place to sleep.

The Moon and Sun had set together, followed by the light from the exploding stars and they were left in complete darkness apart from the light from the fire. It was a very beautiful evening; the stars were shining particularly brightly, as though God was truly smiling on them, giving them all a feeling of comfort and security. Some people were standing staring upwards, gazing at the stars, trying to figure out what was happening in the heavenlies. The vastness of His greatness was displayed before their very eyes; His wonders to behold.

*

"So, what do you think is going to happen in the morning?" asked Charles; one arm around Lisa and the other around both boys; all snuggled under a blanket.

"I have no idea!" said Lisa, "But I know a man who does! He's called Yahshua!" They all laughed. "Come on let's pray

16

together!" Lisa bowed her head and they all followed suit; the boys with hands together. She began,

"Father Yahweh, I come to you in Yahshua's name and ask you to keep us all safe tonight. Keep the little ones warm, Father and send your Angels to guard over your people. Bless you, Father and thank you for your endless love. Amen." With that they all snuggled up and went to sleep.

In the morning Lisa woke, opened her eyes, gasped and let out a small squeal of joy. She could see with her natural eyes. Even though the first thing she saw was Charles, snoring with his mouth wide open, making an incredible noise, she thanked Yahweh for what she witnessed and kissed Charles on the forehead which made him splutter for a second and then reluctantly open his eyes with a squint. He stretched and yawned, then suddenly sprung up as he noticed Lisa staring into his eyes. He cried,

"You can see! Oh, praise God! When did it come back?" Lisa replied,

"Just as I woke up and my vision is better than ever!" They hugged each other.

"Fantastic!" exclaimed Charles, waking the boys and Sophie in the process who soon figured out what was going on and joined in the 'family' hugs.

It was a beautiful day, the birds were singing merrily, and the sun was shining brightly in the sky, next to a full moon. The flash from Orion was over to the far right of the sky, well away from the rising sun but glowing just as bright. For the first time Lisa was able to see the strange light that was being emitted from the heavenlies. It was brighter than usual, and everyone had two shadows. It was very strange; but at the same time, it was a constant reminder of the days they were living in.

"Charles," said Lisa, "I'm just going to take a walk up the mountain, I need to pray. Do you want to come with me?" Charles replied,

"Well, I'm going to try and find some food for us all to eat, so I'll meet you down here when you get back." Lisa turned to the boys and asked,

"How about you guys?" She only had to ask once and without further ado Lisa, Sophie and the boys set off up the hillside. As they were walking Lisa heard a voice say to her,

"Go up to Vantage Point!" So, she said to Sophie,

"Let's go up to Vantage point! From there we'll see what's happening in the city." It was a tough trek through the woods to the rocky outcrop they all called 'Vantage point' but the view there was incredible and on a clear day as it was that day you could see all over the Hightown area and could just about make out the tall buildings in Tolchester. Luke and Josh loved a walk to the 'rocks'; it was always an adventure for them.

As they scrambled to the top of Vantage point and caught their breath from the climb, they stood upright to look at what was always an incredible view. They focused for a couple of seconds and looked out across Hightown.

The sight that met their eyes took them by complete surprise. They all stood in silence with mouths open as they took in the vista. The earthquake had caused absolute devastation. They could see numerous buildings on fire and lots more smouldering, having been put out to some degree. Lights were flashing all over the ravaged town from the emergency service vehicles who were obviously trying their best to deal with the carnage. Plumes of water from fire engines were spraying into the infernos to what seemed like very little or no effect. The town was in such a mess that it was hardly recognisable.

As they looked further out to the left towards Tolchester or 'big town' as the boys used to call it, there were no tall buildings standing; all they could see was dense black smoke.

"Should we send out a rescue party, Lisa?" Sophie asked. Lisa didn't reply. She had her eyes fixed on something as she gazed out to sea. Then she said calmly but firmly,

"Do you see what I think I'm seeing, Sophie?" Sophie replied,

"What's that, Lisa?"

"Look out to sea!" Lisa exclaimed, "What is that blue line across the horizon?!"

They both stared out to sea. "I wish we'd bought some binoculars!" said Lisa. Sophie flapped her hands and shouted,

"Luke has some in his belt pack!"

"Oh well done, Luke!" Lisa said to him as she opened his little hip bag to reveal a small and cheap but nevertheless very useful pair of binoculars. Luke felt totally pleased with himself being so useful. Josh gave him a little shove for being such a 'clever clogs'. Lisa focused the spyglasses on the horizon.

"No!" she cried, "It's! Here, take a look!" She passed them to Sophie.

"Oh, my goodness!" screamed Sophie, "Its a Tsunami! It's heading straight for Hightown!"

"We have to warn everybody we can!" shouted Lisa already starting the descent, "Come on boy's! let's go!"

As they ran down the hillside towards the farm, Lisa shouted to Sophie,

"Did you tell your parents about the Ark?" Sophie replied,

"They wouldn't come, Lisa! They told me they thought you were crazy! I kept trying to call them! I tried again yesterday and last night, but I haven't been able to get a signal since the earthquake!"

"It's been the same for everyone, Sophie." replied Lisa. She looked at Sophie. Their eyes starting to well up with tears. Lisa cried as she realised what that meant. The families, the friendships, the relationships, the families about to be ripped apart again and for many with a fatal conclusion.

Tears were streaming down both their faces as they ran, trying to get to the people as fast as they could. But what could they do?! How could they help? They had been warning people for months in the newspapers, on the radio, on TV and in person. Most had called them 'cranks' or a 'cult'. They had warned many thousands of people but only a few hundred had listened. It was so painful to think how many people must have already died with the earthquake but even more devastating to think of how many were going to die within the next hour.

They screamed at the top of their voices as they ran down the hill towards the yard. Charles came running up to meet them.

"Lisa! What's the matter!" He shouted. Lisa screamed at him,

"There's a Tsunami coming! It's going to hit Hightown! It's huge! Get everyone get up on high ground!" They would surely be okay up there at the farm, but it was better to be safe than sorry.

Charles sounded the alarm to everyone around him and within a few minutes people were starting to climb the hill at the back of the house. Charles ran back up to Lisa and the boys who were on the meadow where they held the feast. Almost out of breath he said to her,

"While you've been gone, lines of people have been arriving here; people you'd talked to at the church and people who heard you on the radio. There must be hundreds still on the way up!"

"We have to warn them too! Hurry!" shouted Lisa. "Sophie can you look after the boys and take them back to Vantage Point?" She hugged her boys and Sophie took them back to where they'd just come from. Charles and Lisa ran past the lines of people winding their way up the mountain, shouting out instructions as they went. They saw Sam on the lower yard and as they ran past him Charles shouted,

"Get everyone up the hill, Sam! There's a tidal wave coming!" Sam panicked for a second and turned one way then the other, not knowing who to warn first. He then screamed at anyone and everyone to get to the high ground.

Charles and Lisa ran past the wreckage of the house and down the driveway telling everyone they passed with increasing urgency. The people on the driveway looked in a state of shock; they were dirty and bedraggled and a lot of them were carrying injuries of some sort. They had suffered terribly in Hightown after the quake but worse, far worse was to come. Lisa wanted to stop and help some people who looked badly injured, but Charles quickly reminded her of what they needed to do. There were hundreds of people stretching out down the driveway. They reached the gates of the Ark and people were still coming up the road towards the main gate. Suddenly she heard a voice in her head saying,

"Turn back now, Lisa! Turn back!"

"I can't!" she thought to herself, "What about all these people?!"

"Lisa, turn back!" the voice said firmer this time.

"I can't!" she screamed. Her legs suddenly stopped running. It was as though she was trying to run through thick treacle.

"Head back my child!" Yahweh persisted. It was no use she couldn't move forward, only back in the direction she had run.

"We have to go back, Charles!" shouted a defeated Lisa, "Tell these people to hurry and to pass the message back!"

Charles went down to line and passed the message on and then caught up with Lisa. They ran back towards the farm; Lisa shouting, "Come on hurry!" to people as they ran back past them. They reached the yard and ushered people up the hill.

A terrible menacing noise like they had never heard before began to come towards them from the coast. The mighty wave was on its way. It was a hideous sound, combining millions of gallons of gushing water, the crashing of buildings being bulldozed over and the tearing down of trees, all in one.

"Come on!!" Lisa screamed at people in unison with Charles, "Run!" The noise was escalating as they ran back across the yard and up to the meadow behind what was once the old house. They could now see the giant wave approaching fast; taking everything with it; devouring acres of land by the second. They stood and watched for a second, almost transfixed by what they were witnessing. It was heading right up the valley towards them. They snapped out of the devastating spectacle, turned and ran higher up the hill. Hundreds of people were trying to make their way up the hill ahead of them, exhausted but still running; running for their very lives, as well as many still behind them.

Lisa screamed as she felt the cool, wet spray of salt water in the air hitting the back of her head. The force of the wave made a terrifying wind like a sea mist in a gale. The sound of the wave was now deafening in their ears, tearing down the forest on the estate.

22

Lisa looked behind again to see the wave crash against the yard, sweeping all kinds of numbers of people with it. She turned her face away, not able to look at the devastation just a few hundred feet away from her but the screams of those taken would never be forgotten.

The water rose up to a level just short of the meadow where they held the feast and their wedding, when suddenly it stopped, paused and began to recede, taking fallen trees, shrubs and all the wreckage from the house and buildings with it, but leaving injured and maimed bodies writhing on the ground, battered and bruised from the ordeal; some clinging to tree stumps or anything solid they could find.

Lisa and Charles continued to climb the mountain to Vantage point where Luke, Josh and Sophie were. When they reached the top, Sam, Ben, Jenny, Jim and Connie were there too. They all looked bemused in disbelief at the destruction in front of them. The surrounding hills had all been stripped of their trees and looked totally bare. Hightown was now part of the sea and was completely underwater. There would certainly be no survivors down there, that was for sure. It was hard to comprehend what they were looking at. It was a true horror scene.

Lisa hugged her boys and checked they were okay, then stood up and looked at the scene of deluge with the others. Apart from the food and belongings people had with them everything was now gone. Behind them stood hundreds of people looking bewildered and dumbfounded; in a state of shock after such a horrific trauma. Lisa looked at them; floods of sorrow washed over her. Tears fell down her cheeks as she gazed over the meadow and the yard. She looked at the others and said,

"We need to go and help the people!"

Wherever they looked people were crying. Many were injured and needed attention, some bleeding badly, others with broken limbs and most were totally exhausted and riddled with shock. People were trying to help one another where they could but many of the injuries were too severe. A couple of nurses were attending to the worst situations, but the demand was far greater than the help they could give, and they had no medical supplies whatsoever. After seeing the extent of all the injuries Lisa pulled away from the crowds and went back to the rock on Vantage point. She needed to pray and get help, or they were going to have trouble on their hands; there must have been more than a hundred people who desperately needed help. She climbed the rock again and knelt down on the top and bowed her head. Before she could say anything, the voice of the living God transcended the hillside. He said, audibly for all to hear,

"Well done, my children!" Lisa climbed down from the rock and lay prostrate on the ground as His presence filled the whole mountainside.

"Do not be afraid, my children!" He said, "You will all be safe! You are my people and I am your God. I am Yahweh Rapha and you are healed!" An overwhelming calmness descended on the hillside and took over from the chaos and screams of pain and replaced it with silence and peace. Lisa got up on her feet and looked across the meadow.

In front of her very eyes, He was healing the people. He was restoring and making them whole right there and then. Cries of astonishment came from people as broken bones came together, twisted limbs corrected themselves and gashes were seared. In sheer amazement Lisa responded by falling to her knees and shouting at the top of her voice,

"You are incredible! Yahweh, I love you!"

The cries of agony that had filled the valley had now changed to shouts of joy and jubilation. Psalm thirty came immediately to Lisa's mind, where David wrote,

"You have turned my mourning into dancing

and my sorrow into joy!"

All around people were applauding, cheering and jumping up and down, praising God with all their might. Then amidst all the celebrations Lisa heard a whisper saying,

"And you, Lisa Michaels must help these people to safety!" She replied,

"Father, where is safe, now that everything has gone?" She heard her Father reply,

"Stand at the crossroads and look! Ask for the ancient path."

"What does that mean?" she asked with some urgency, but this time heard no reply.

She stood up on her feet and looked around at the jubilant scene before her. It made her smile again in wonderment at the greatness of Yahweh. Then she looked down towards the house and the yard which instantly changed her emotion. It was such a sad scene. She remembered how they had all been so excited to move there and now it was all gone.

The wave had swept it all clean and all she could see was the stone slab that the old house had been built on. She looked back at the yard. Then at the area where the buildings once stood, then back to the house. Something she hadn't noticed before and could see now everything was gone, was that the paths from the buildings, the driveway and the lane to the fields, all converged right in front of the old house. There were four tracks in all and from where she stood they looked like the cross. She looked again and turn her head slightly to one side. It was almost a perfect cross. She said to herself,

"It's a crossroads."

Then it hit her like a bolt of lightning.

"That's it!" she shouted, "Stand at the crossroads and look!" She ran down the hill, to the field.

"Charles!" she shouted out, "Where are you?!"

"I'm here, Lisa!" He shouted back in return, enjoying the celebrations, "Isn't this great!"

"Yes," she replied, "it's fantastic but I need you to come and look at something with me!" He followed her down to the yard which was still soaked from the wave. She stood in the middle of the yard in front of where the house was; the centre point of the four tracks, as she had seen from the Vantage Point and said,

"So, I'm at the crossroads! Now look!" She couldn't see anything. "Charles, what can you see?"

"Not a lot!" He replied, "Everything has gone!"

"Okay," she thought, "Now I ask!" She smiled and said out loud,

"Where is the ancient path?" She expected a reply but didn't get one. She turned around slowly, searching intently as she did. When she faced the old house she heard,

"Stop!" She was staring directly at the path up to the place where the old house stood. She shouted to her hubby,

"Charles! It's here!" Charles replied,

"What is?!" Lisa answered,

"I don't know but it's here!" Charles looked at her with a puzzled expression. She continued, "Could you have a look on the foundation of the old house and see if you can see anything!" Charles jumped up onto the stone slab which the lovely old house used to stand on. He looked around.

"Can't find anything here, Lisa!" he shouted back, "…. Apart from these old wooden planks!" Lisa climbed up to join him on the standing of the old house, which was beautifully constructed from old stone blocks. She jumped on the wooden planks. Charles added his weight to the argument and jumped with her. The planks seemed to move a little. They jumped again and looked at each other.

"Does that sound a bit hollow to you?" Lisa asked.

"Let's have a look!" Charles replied. "Hmm, could be! Let's get them up and find out!" Just then Sam came wandering down from the field, looking around at the landscape; a little confused and bewildered but very happy nevertheless. Charles saw him and shouted,

"Hey Sam, just the man! Come and give me a hand!"

A slightly beleaguered Sam stood on the crossroads of the paths and remarked,

"Look at all this! Can you believe it! All that hard work just washed away! What was it all for?"

"I know just how you feel, Sam!" replied Lisa, "But Yahweh has a plan! I just know it!"

"Amen!" responded Charles, "Now come and help us with this, Sam!"

They couldn't get the planks to budge.

It's no use!" said Sam straining with the effort, "We need something to lever them out with!" They looked around and eventually found an old metal bar that the wave had left behind that looked like it could do the job.

It was a real struggle; they were more like beams than planks and seemed like they had been there a very long time. Also, they had being soaked with the water from the wave, which had made them tighter and heavier still. After much persistence, one of the planks began to lift and eventually with much effort popped up. The pressure was released and the second of the planks came up much easier. Sure enough, they were covering a hole, which Sam and Charles duly stuck their heads into.

"What's that?!" Charles exclaimed peering into the darkness.

"I think we have found some steps!" said Sam, "It must have been an old cellar or something!" They wrestled and struggled with the four remaining planks and then all three of them stood, arms folded, staring into the hole; admiring their efforts like a group of workmen.

There was indeed a set of steps leading down. They all stared at the bottom of the steps. It was very overgrown, thick with old briers but surely, they must lead somewhere?

Charles went down the steps first, followed by Lisa and then Sam. Charles used the bar of metal to chop down the briers and creepers that had amassed over the years since the steps had last been used.

"Well, well!" Just look at this!" said Charles pulling aside the last creepers and cobwebs, "Its a door!"

Lisa and Sam watched Charles clear the overgrowth. There were far too many prickles and cobwebs for either of them to be willing to go any further. As far as Lisa was concerned, where there are cobwebs, there are spiders and as she always said, "Spiders are an abomination." Sam was of the same thought. They shuddered in unison as Charles got stuck in. When the way was clear, Charles stood back and they all looked at the door. There appeared to be a sign of some description in the middle of the door. Charles wiped the dust of what seemed like many years away.

It read......

'To the Ark.'

Chapter Three

Through the Door

The door was large and made of solid Oak. It had metal rivets through it for strength and intricate metalwork for decoration. It rested on huge ornate hinges and had a large keyhole with a forged handle just above it. It had obviously been made a long time ago and made to shut something very special in or keep something bad out.

Charles continued to dust it off as the others just stared at the beauty of this thing. They all looked at each other not saying a word but asking the same questions in their heads. What secrets was this door keeping from the world and what did it have to do with their future?

Charles looked at Lisa and Sam and reached for the handle. He turned it. It was locked.

He tried it again just in case it was stiff with age.

"No way!" exclaimed Charles, now pulling at the door. It wasn't going to budge.

"We need a key!" cried Sam, "Or an axe!"

They stepped back from the door to think of a solution.

"What kind of key would open this?" Charles asked. Then it struck Lisa.

"Oh no!" said Lisa, "There's a bunch of keys I was given with the house! One of them was a big one that I couldn't find a lock for. I put them in my desk!" Then the realisation hit them that her desk of course had been washed away with the remains of the house.

"I hadn't had a chance to salvage everything!" said Charles, "It must have been under all the rubble!"

They walked back up the steps and onto the yard to re-group their thoughts and figure out a way of opening that old door, when Lisa stopped dead in her tracks.

"What was that?! Listen!" she exclaimed.

"I can't hear anything!" replied Charles.

"Me neither!" said Sam.

"Shush!" insisted Lisa, "There it goes again!" She followed the sound that she could hear and walked across the yard to the other side of where the food plant once stood.

"Hello!" voices called feebly, "Help us!"

Lisa quickly jumped over what remained of the uprooted foundation of the building to find two people huddled together.

"Hey guys! Are you okay?" Lisa said in a soft caring voice, "You're safe now." They lifted their bloody, soiled heads. Lisa recognised them immediately and stroked their matted hair. It was a dazed, bedraggled and confused looking Tom and Jan Philips. Lisa lifted her head up and beckoned,

"Charles! Sam! Come here quickly!" They only had a few cuts and bruises but they were totally traumatised having suffered so much over the last twenty-four hours. Tom tried to explain in a shaky voice how they were hit by the wave and carried off by it, then thrown out of it and dumped in the woods.

31

"We were off to help some friends! We thought we'd be safe and that God would take care of us!" He said in a feeble, quivering voice. Lisa replied,

"I think He has taken good care of you! You are alive, and He's brought you to us. Now you'll be okay!"

Sam and Charles helped them slowly to their feet and dusted them down. They were trembling with shock and shivering with cold. They were immaculately dressed as always, Tom still sporting a tie, although now completely dirty and drenched through. As they began to slowly walk with them, something caught Lisa's eye, in what remained of the South woods. She did a double take and exclaimed under her breath,

"It can't be!" She looked harder and immediately ran off, in the direction of the woods, leaving a puzzled Charles and Sam to look after their latest guests, wondering what had got into her. She stumbled through the roots and stumps of the ripped up and snapped off trees as fast as she could.

She stopped when she reached her destination.

"No way!" she cried with total excitement. She ran her hands over smooth veneered wood. It was her desk! Unbelievably, looking remarkably intact, albeit on its side.

"Wow Father!" she shouted out loud, "You've done it again! You are astonishing!" She struggled as she pulled it over onto its legs and slid open the top centre drawer. She scrambled around in the drawer pushing things to the left and right. Her hand felt something heavy which she knew was the big key she had never found a home for. A smile came to her face followed by pure joy as she took the key out. She thought to herself,

"This had to be it! What else could it be?"

32

She took it out and stared at it. It was just a plain old brass key but was this the key to their future. She waved at Charles and Sam back at the yard. They could see her jumping up and down but had no idea why she was acting so strange. She ran back to join them on the yard, waving the key above her head triumphantly. She looked at them, smiled confidently and said,

"How great is our God?! Eh?!"

"No way!" shouted Sam and Charles together jumping up and down in excitement. Tom and Jan, not having a clue what was going on, didn't say a word but tried to look pleased for Lisa.

"Sam, would you take Tom and Jan up onto the top meadow to see one of the nurses there," Lisa continued, "then hurry back down and we'll try the door!" Sam took the dishevelled couple off up the path to the meadow while Charles and Lisa went up on the stone slab of the old house again and down the steps to the door.

It seemed to 'welcome' them as they approached it, key in hand and somehow it looked much cleaner and newer than it did before. They stood in front of the door and looked at the key in Lisa's hand. It had a small inscription on it that Lisa had never noticed before. In truth she hadn't taken much notice of the key because it didn't have a purpose before. On it was engraved, 'Is 26.2'. They looked at each other. Lisa said,

"We need a bible!" Lisa handed the key to Charles who put it in the door. It turned like a well-oiled machine, which was surprising considering how old it looked. The bolt made a loud 'thunk' as it slid across and unlocked. Charles turned the handle and pushed the door. They stared at each other, both having a concerned but excited look on their faces.

The door made an archetypal creak as it opened, dragging a little on the ground. Charles put his head inside the door. It was totally black inside and a little too creepy with far too much potential for spiders for Lisa's liking. He opened it wider to let more light in but still everything inside looked totally black. He stepped through the door and Lisa followed precariously. Sam came running down the steps and scared the 'living daylights' out of both of them.

"Sorry!" whispered Sam knowing what he'd done by the look on their faces, "I was just excited to get back!"

Their heartbeats returned to normal and they walked into the darkness, Charles leading the way, into what seemed like a long corridor that had been somehow cut out of the bedrock. It was amazing to think that whatever they were now in, wherever they were, was directly underneath the house they'd lived in. They took a few more tentative steps into the tunnel. The darkness was so intense that they couldn't see a hand in front of their faces. Lisa whispered,

"Charles, let me go first, I've got used to doing this!" She wondered if this was why Yahweh had left her blind for longer than the others. She used her hearing and mind's eye again just as she had done before. Charles looked back. He could see the door, but the light didn't seem to penetrate through the pitch black.

"What was that?!" whispered Sam, terrified by the whole episode.

"What was what?" replied Charles.

"That sound!" answered Sam.

"What sound? I didn't hear anything!" Charles insisted.

"Oh! It must have been me then!" replied Sam.

"What? You made the noise?" questioned Charles.

"You two!? Behave yourselves!" laughed Lisa.

They continued on, into the darkness, feeling like explorers in a lost world. As they turned a slight bend, they suddenly saw some light. It was a strip of light low to the ground. They got closer and could see light flickering through the gap underneath what looked like a closed door. They approached the door realising that something or someone must be creating that light on the other side. Lisa grabbed Charles' arm and pointed to a doorknob. Charles took hold of the doorknob and gave it a turn. The latch released, and he slowly opened the door a few inches to reveal the source of the light. As Charles peeped through the gap he could see that the light was coming from a lit fire in a fireplace. Bravely, Charles opened the door wider to reveal a sight which immediately took their breath and caused Sam to turn and run. Next to the fire on an old wooden chair sat an old man who was sobbing quietly, wearing an old dusty prayer shawl draped over his head. Charles and Lisa cautiously stepped into the room and stared at the old man. Sam came back when he realised that Charles and Lisa were still alive and that he was very alone in a very dark corridor. The flickering light from the fire dimly lit up the whole room. The walls were filled, floor to ceiling with bookshelves full of old books and there was one solitary table with a battered tin plate on it. The old man; taking no notice of the three of them, just kept weeping, seemingly totally oblivious that he had company. Nobody said a word; it felt like a dream. Questions raced through Lisa's head;

"Who was this?"

"How long had he been down there?"

She plucked up some courage and slowly approached the man. She crouched down in front of him and placed her hand on his shoulder to comfort him. As she touched him, dust sprung up from the prayer shawl that he wore; he had obviously been there a while.

She expected him to look at her, but he just kept on crying, tears streaming down his well-lined face. She spoke to the man,

"Hello." she said, "Are you alright?"

There was no reply just tears. She asked again,

"Why are you crying, Sir?" Still he just kept weeping. She tried again to get a response and said, "Are you hungry, are you thirsty, are you cold? Is there anything we can do for you?"

Suddenly, he spoke, which caused Sam to half turn and run again.

"Why are they so blind!" he said in a sad, gravely but kind voice, "Why can't they see what they're doing!" Lisa was just going to ask him who he was referring to when he continued,

"I carry a burden, too much for one soul to bear. It is time. It is upon the whole earth and yet the sheep are led astray by the shepherds. Bring them back! Bring them back!" he wept. He paused, hung his head for a second or two then lifted it and looked Lisa in the eyes. He continued,

"They teach lawlessness, they cast aside the commands of the Most High, believing the Saviour's sacrifice made obsolete the eternal words of The Holy One. But hear these words; People must do the will of Almighty Yahweh! He will settle for nothing less. He loves his children so, but they do not listen. I cry His tears." He started to cry again. Lisa tried to console him. She bent towards his ear and whispered,

"We are here for Him. We have seen His face!" she paused, "We only desire to do the Fathers will. We have been sent by Mr Carter to this place to carry it out." He looked at Lisa through his reddened, tear-filled eyes and the corners of his mouth almost smiled. He tried to stand up. Lisa helped him to his feet. He folded the shawl from on top of his head to his shoulders to reveal his long grey hair, matted and dusty with time. He beckoned Charles to join them. Sam stood at the door looking on. The old man turned Charles to face Lisa and took hold of both their right hands. Shakily, he loosely wrapped a plaited cord around their wrists and placed a small scroll tied with a string on top of their upturned hands. He turned to one then the other and said,

"I have waited many seasons for you and now this is your time. I pass this on to you. This mantle is yours," He took off the prayer shawl from his shoulders and placed it around both of their shoulders and said,

"For the eyes of Yahweh roam throughout the earth to show Himself strong for those whose hearts are completely His." He paused and looked at them in turn, saying;

"Charles you are as David, a man after Gods own heart. Lisa you are as Noah, willing to stand for what is right and good, even if you should stand alone." It immediately struck them both that he somehow knew their names. He continued,

"Charles you are as John, a voice calling out in the wilderness, preparing the way! Lisa you are as Esther, you will know the keys to the release of the Children of the Most High.
You will both raise children who will be witnesses to the Holy One of Israel, the Most High Elohim."

He closed his old eyes and prayed, "Father, put these words on their minds and write them on their hearts. In Yahshua's name. Amen"

The scroll on their hands suddenly appeared to melt in front of their eyes, then completely dissolved into their skin and further into their veins. The old man unwrapped their hands and hugged them both. He took hold of their hands, looked them both in the eyes and said,

37

"Because of lawlessness, many do not know the call on their lives. The power of the Most High is sealed within the Words of Truth. His children cry out for the promises of the covenant, yet the key to them is cast aside because of the deceiver. Go tell them! Tell them to return quickly, that they may be counted worthy to escape that which is coming upon the earth. Time is running out, but it is not too late, for though you see the end, it is not yet, but is yet to come!"

He leaned towards them and whispered,

"My job is done now, thank you!"

They hugged again.

Sam couldn't believe his eyes. He stood there watching this whole thing with his mouth wide open. What had he just witnessed?

"Incredible to see isn't it!" said a voice from behind him, in a broken-English accent.

"It is!" said Sam, mesmerised by the beauty of what he had just seen. Then he suddenly realized that there was someone behind him and every hair on his body stood up. A hand rested on his shoulder and he 'jumped out of his skin.' He turned around to see Eli, the angel, grinning at him through the darkness.

"Eli!" Sam screamed, "You terrified me!"

Everybody laughed. Eli came into the room and everyone embraced.

"Eli! It's so great to see you!" cried Lisa, "Are you back with us?"

He replied, "I'm not, I'm afraid, Lisa. I've just come for Ezra here," He pointed to the Old Man and continued, "He has wept long enough. He is going home." He smiled at Lisa and Charles. "It's so good to see you guys again!" he continued, "What an amazing place Mr Carter built here, have you seen it all yet?"

"No not yet!" replied Lisa, "This was our first stop."

"Well," continued Eli, "you will all be safe here and He will supply all your needs. Praise His Glorious Name!"

"Will everyone fit in here, Eli?" Lisa asked with concern, "We have many with us!" Eli replied smiling,

"Oh, many fold, Lisa, many fold! Anyway, we have to go now, I bid you good day and we will both see you soon."

Before they could even answer, Eli took the hand of old man Ezra and they lifted off the ground and disappeared into the ether, before their very eyes. There was a moment of silence.

"Did that just happen?" said Charles.

"I think so!" replied Lisa.

"I'm not so sure!" answered Sam. They all laughed in amazement.

"How about the scroll, Lisa?!" Charles remarked, "Wasn't that amazing? Did you feel it?"

"Oh yes!" replied Lisa, "That was what you would call supernatural impartation!"

"And his name was Ezra!" Charles exclaimed, "Do you think he's the Ezra from the bible?"

"I have no idea!" Lisa replied, "But surely a prophet!"

Sam just looked at them both without saying anything. He glanced around the room and noticed that there was a lantern on a shelf and wondered if it worked. They tried to light it with a spill from the fire and sure enough, it worked perfectly.

The room was amazing. There were books everywhere; a study extraordinaire; a delvers paradise.

"There must be a bible in here somewhere?" said Lisa looking at the shelves.

"Here on the table!" exclaimed Charles and handed it to Lisa.

"What is engraved on the key, Charles?" she said opening the pages of the old worn bible. He replied looking at the key,

"It says, 'Is 26.2', which has to be Isaiah 26 verse 2." She flicked through the delicate leaves and stopped at the appropriate place, turned one or two more pages and stopped again and read. Her mouth gaped. She looked up at Charles and Sam then back to the bible and read,

"Open ye the gates, that the righteous nation that keepeth the truth may enter in," She looked back at Charles, then at Sam.

"This place! The door!" she exclaimed. "Could we be that righteous nation!?" Nobody said a word. They just looked at each other. Charles broke the silence,

"Shall we go and explore? Eli said there was much more to see!"

They all agreed, and Sam picked up the lantern and led the way.

They walked out into the darkness of the corridor. It didn't seem quite so 'spooky' anymore; God was surely with them.

They wandered down the corridor passing several other doors that they decided they would investigate later as they wanted to see the full extent of this underground refuge.

The corridor eventually began to widen, and they suddenly found themselves in a cavern as big as a cathedral.

Looking around from side to side and up and down, Sam said,

"We had better go find ourselves some more people! This place is immense!"

"Let's go and get the people we already have!" Lisa said excitedly.

"But how are we going to be able to see?" Asked Sam.

Charles responded, "I can't imagine that old Mr Carter would have built all of this and not solved the light situation! Let's check out those other rooms and see what's in there. Then we can get the people!"

So, they wandered back up the long corridor and sure enough in the rooms they had passed there were supplies galore. They found lanterns, stoves, pans, tin cups and plates stacked up to the ceilings! It was incredible! A prepper's dream! They even found something to eat, although they were only what Charles described as survival biscuits in little sealed packets, there were crates of them. They figured they could hand out to everyone to quench the immediate hunger situation. Sam tried one and although he claimed they had an 'acquired' taste, they were very thankful for them. Lisa commented while munching on a biscuit,

"When we run out of these we will be totally dependent on God, but I know He will provide!" The others agreed.

They lit a bunch of the lanterns and exposed more of the main cavern. It was fabulous, and it felt so warm too. On the far side they could make out a waterfall running down the wall of the cavern.

"Praise Yahweh!" shouted Charles, "Drinking water!" They dashed over to the water to try it out. It tasted so good; better than any they had ever tasted before.

It was time to go and get the people and show then their new home. They walked back to the entrance and up the steps.

They screened their eyes and squinted as they adjusted to the brightness of the sunlight.

People were still sitting on the grass in the meadow talking in groups, enjoying the sunny weather. Lisa could see Ben, Jenny, Jim, Connie, Carol and their 'adopted' daughter, Sophie with the boys in tow, encouraging all the new people that had recently arrived there. Considering the ups and downs that had taken place in the last twenty-four hours, everyone was in great spirit. Charles went to get Ben and Jim, while Lisa grabbed the girls and they all met together on the yard. Lisa explained everything to the group who stood and listened in amazement. Jenny shouted,

"I knew Yahweh wouldn't let us down!" There was rounds of "Amen!" and "HalleluYah!" going off all over.

Lisa went with Charles to talk to all the people about their new sleeping arrangements while Sam took the leaders down the steps and into the Ark to get the place ready for the people to come down.

Charles and Lisa gathered people together which felt like a scene from the great exodus out of Egypt in the days of Moses albeit on a much smaller scale, but still very impressive and in many ways just as miraculous. Lisa took the hands of Tom and Jan Philips and led them personally down the hill. They both tried to explain all the reasons for their behaviour towards Lisa and what had happened with Pastor Adams, but Lisa interrupted them,

"I never even think about it!" She replied, "We're all God's children and we love you!"

Everyone was organised to form a long line and they began to filter down to the Ark. Watching them slowly go down the steps and through the door, Lisa cuddled Charles' arm.

"The adventure continues!" she said looking up into his eyes. Charles sighed contentedly,

"Yes, my darling! Exciting times."

The Sun and Moon were starting to go down when the last person went in.

Charles and Lisa followed. He closed the big door, put the big key in the lock and turned it, locking them all in. They had a new home.

Chapter Four

Seek and You will find

Biscuits, mugs and plates were handed out to everyone as they entered the main cavern, which looked amazing, now it was all lit up. The work that God and Old Mr Carter together had done there was breath-taking and by the minute, it seemed, people were making new discoveries. Many small corridors led from the main cavern to individual 'rooms' which were complete with a straw matting to sleep on. It seemed that nothing had been forgotten. There were even areas screened off for people to wash and bathe at the lower end of the stream, near the waterfall. They had no immediate supply of food, other than the biscuits but their faith that Yahweh would provide was strong.

This place was a true haven and people knew that they could survive there; at least for a time. Since the healings the faith of many had multiplied and Lisa and the others wasted no time in getting to know the new people and making them feel at home.

The Ark was to be their refuge; a safe place away from the tribulation that had begun to happen in the outside world. This place, they hoped, was going to keep them away from the calamities that they knew were coming upon the earth.

Lisa recalled from her years of bible study that the earth would protect Yahweh's people. In chapter twelve verse six of the book of Revelation, she remembered it said that "the woman (Israel) fled to the wilderness to a place prepared by her God where she may be taken care of for one thousand two hundred and sixty days or three and a half years. She also recalled the earth helping the woman and the dragon being enraged and waging war with those who obey God's commandments and hold to the testimony of Yahshua. Bible prophecy was coming to pass before their very eyes and even though they could all have a real feeling of security there at the Ark, Lisa knew that there were people who didn't know their bibles and they needed to be made aware of the troubled times that were ahead so that they didn't lose faith when trials came.

The following morning Lisa was carefully tidying up in Ezra's room with Jenny, dusting off what seemed like years of accumulated dust and trying to make some sort of order of the bookshelves.

"I've noticed," said Jenny, "that this fire is always lit! Do you get cold in here or something?" Lisa smiled and said,

"Not at all! We've never touched it! I believe Yahweh is showing us that His Spirit is with us! It was lit when we found Ezra here!"

"That's amazing!" replied Jenny opening the door to shake off her rag. As she did they noticed something of a commotion going on down the corridor towards the entrance.

"I'll go and see what's going on!" said Jenny leaving Lisa clearing up what seemed like centuries of mess. Jenny returned in no time at all,

"Lisa!" she said excitedly, "There's more people! Ben found them wandering around on the yard!" Lisa rushed out of the room and ran to meet the new arrivals. She recognised them immediately as the Pugh family; a family from her church in Hightown who had been jeering at her on the day Christopher Adams humiliated them publicly. Although she was aware of the hatred they had for her that day, the spirit inside her took over and instantly wiped away any ill feeling she may have had towards them.

"Oh, you poor things!" she cried as she hugged the little ones, "Come on in and get warm. We'll find you some dry clothing and something to eat. I'll take you to meet Connie and Jim, they will get you tidied up and find you somewhere to rest." This family had been out for a drive and somehow the wave picked their car up off the road and deposited it in a safe place to one side of the giant swath similar to Tom and Jan although they didn't get any injuries. It had been quite miraculous, and the Pugh family felt that they must have been meant for something else other than death. They remembered Lisa and her time at the church open day and the opposition she had faced. They also remembered where she had said the Ark was and so headed that way when God so mercifully plucked them from danger.

Lisa and Jenny led them down the corridor to the main cavern and left them with Connie and Jim before heading back to Ezra's room to carry on with their work. Something in Lisa wanted to be angry with those people for the way they had treated her at the church and yet submitting herself to the Spirit of Yahweh had enabled her to extinguish any unforgiveness in a flash. It was something she hadn't really known before, but it was truly amazing.

"Wow all these people coming here Lisa." said Jenny as she dusted the mantle piece, "Praise Yahweh for their souls!" Lisa agreed with a smile and sunk her head back into a little book she had found. After studying the contents for a few minutes, she beckoned to Jenny and said,

"Hey Jenny! Come and look at this!" Jenny put her duster down and looked over Lisa's shoulder,

"What is it?" she asked. Lisa replied,

"It's a book written by Old Mr Carter! It seems to be talking about a type of food that grows down here! Can you believe it!?" She looked at Jenny. "There is a plant that can grow down here!" They sat down at the table and looked at the book together, amazed at what they were reading. Lisa continued,

"Every morning Old Mr Carter and his teams of workers down here used to eat the leaves of this plant, which according to Old Mr Carter was delicious!" She looked at Jenny with a smile, "Oh Jenny, this is the answer! This is what Yahweh has provided for us down here! Almost like the provision of Manna in the desert for the Israelites!"

"This is amazing!" cried Jenny, "And apparently they're delicious!" They laughed and praised God.

"Come on!" laughed Lisa, "Let's go and find it!"

Lisa walked through the corridors with a broad smile on her face. The only thing she'd had concerns about in the Ark, was food but Yahweh had come through again. Now they were on the search. They met Connie on the way and their friend from the radio station, Sharon Long. They explained what they were looking for and the four of them continued the search, hunting high and low. Every nook and cranny were looked in but still they couldn't find any plant life whatsoever. Sam joined the hunt.

"Plants growing down here?" He said half joking, "This has to be from God!" Suddenly Jenny cried out,

"HalleluYah!"

Lisa looked up to where she heard God's name being praised and saw Jenny crawling on a ledge about ten feet up from the cavern floor on the east side, opposite the waterfall.

"What are you doing up there, Jenny?" shouted Lisa

"Picking leaves!" replied Jenny victoriously, "I've found them! Come up here and have a look!"

"How did you get up there?!" laughed Lisa.

"There's a ramp at the far end!" replied Jenny, "Hurry up!"

Lisa, Connie and Sharon ran over to the ramp and walked onto the ledge where Jenny was.

"Look!" pointed Jenny. Over to the left there was thousands upon thousands of tiny plants with diamond shaped leaves about an inch in diameter.

"He was right, Lisa!" said Jenny still chewing, "They are delicious!" They picked a bunch of them each and took them down to the cavern and on to the store where the little stoves were. Connie was particularly pleased as she had always been the principle cook at the Ark and now she had her job back again.

They found they could eat them raw or steam them like spinach and accompany anything that was found above ground. They tasted fabulous. The smell wafted through into the great cavern and pretty soon a hungry crowd had gathered around. Lisa came out of the store with a large smile on her face and shouted to everyone who could hear.

"Right everyone! Let's eat!" Strangely as soon as she mentioned food the men came running. Suddenly there was Charles, Ben and Jim wanting to know what they had discovered and more to the point how it tasted. Lisa felt a real ease in her spirit; they now had something that would be able to keep them all alive. Even if they got bored of eating leaves at least they wouldn't die of starvation.

*

Lisa wandered through the passages and corridors checking that people were settling down. They had all found a place that they could call their home. It was amazing to see how peaceful the Ark could be, considering how many people were down there now. They all had their own space with their private rooms and all the provisions of a relatively normal life.

It was tempting to hold a role call and see exactly how many people were with them now, but Lisa was reminded of the story of King David counting his fighting men and so thought better of it. She saw Jenny and Sharon who had been doing the rounds just as she was and they all concluded that their work was done for the day and that they should go and try to get some sleep with the rest of them. It was difficult to feel tired due to there being no night and day as such. Most people would tend to sleep just when they felt like sleeping but that day they all seemed to be tired together.

Lisa went back to her room, checked the boys, then climbed into bed and snuggled up next to her hubby. Their married life, so far had been extremely different to how she had always imagined, but she knew that God had great things planned for them both. She kissed Charles on the cheek and cuddled up behind him, safe and sound.

When Lisa woke, she could hear something of a disturbance going on. It was Jenny talking with Ben outside her room. Lisa got up and went to the door.

"There's something we need to tell you, Lisa." said Jenny.

"Okay," Lisa replied, "do you want to go to the office?"

"No, it's fine." said Ben, "It's just that there's someone at the door!"

"So, let them in!" Lisa replied, "The more the merrier!"

"This is different, Lisa!" Jenny continued, "It's Christopher Adams!" She paused and looked at Lisa who said nothing in response. Jenny explained,

"There was a knock on the door; I opened it; saw who it was and immediately shut it again. But I'm sure he will still be there cos he looked so battered!"

Lisa just looked at Jenny and Ben, then turned around and went back into her room. The feeling of anger that was immediately taken away when the Pugh family arrived was proving more difficult to shift with the thought of allowing Adams into their midst. Was Yahweh trying to warn her of something?

She paced around the room then went over to the bed and shook Charles, who spluttered a little before gaining 'Compos Mentis'.

"What's wrong? He said a little blurry eyed. Lisa's answer to his question cleared his mind instantly. He cried in response,

"You have to be kidding? The nerve of that man!"

"We have to let him in, Charles! It's the only thing we can do!"

"Are you sure?" Charles replied, "Have you forgotten what he did to you?" The pictures of his public humiliation of Lisa and the boys; the assault in the house and him pointing a gun in her face came rushing back into her mind. She responded,

"Of course, I haven't! How can I ever forget those things!? But he is a human! We have to let him in!" They looked at each other eye to eye. "Can you go and let him in, Charles and bring him to Ezra's room? I'll go and get the others."

As Charles walked up the corridor, he was dreading seeing the man who had caused so much pain in his wife's life, but he knew it was the only thing they could do. He approached the door. There was a timid tap on the huge oak timbers of the only defence system the Ark had.

"Who is there?!" Charles asked knowingly.

A feeble voice replied,

"It's me, Pastor Christopher Adams! Can I come in?!"

Charles opened the door.

A sorry sight met Charles' eyes. This man certainly had taken quite a battering. He was cut and bruised, and his clothes were blood stained, dirty and soaking wet. He was sat on the steps looking up at Charles.

"Please, help me!" He pleaded feebly. Charles took him by his cold, damp arm and helped him to his feet.

"Come on, Mr Adams, let's get you inside." said Charles with compassion. He led him slowly down the corridor.

"I'm Charles, by the way; Lisa's husband."

"You must hate me!" spluttered Adams. Charles replied,

"I didn't like what you did, but I don't hate you."

They arrived at the office door and walked in. Lisa stood there with the rest of the team and looked at the pitiful sight before their eyes. An ashamed looking Adams hung his head and just stood there as though in the dock; a far cry from the arrogant man they knew so well. Charles introduced everyone to him.

"And this, of course, is my wife Lisa!" leaving her until last.

As Lisa walked over to greet Mr. Adams, a voice spoke quietly in her ear:

"He will betray you when he gets the chance, but so will others! Adams will help you separate the 'wheat from the chaff' quicker than if you allow others to fester by themselves. Not all at the Ark will be saved."

"Yes, we've met, thank you Charles!" responded Lisa. "Welcome to the Ark, Mr Adams, and, how are you? I haven't seen you in quite a while."

"I'm okay, under the circumstances! I'm alive anyway!" he replied softly which was not like him, "Having lost everything I ever worked for!" He paused, "But thank you for allowing me to stay here."

Lisa smiled and continued,

"We'll get a room ready for you and get you some food, if you're hungry?"

"Thank you" he replied, "I'm very hungry." He paused and hung his head, then lifted it and continued sorrowfully, fighting back tears,

"I'm so sorry, Lisa, for all the misunderstanding we've had in the past. I was so out of order, I can hardly believe it, please forgive me!" Ben interrupted from the other side of the room,

"Yes, and we'll forgive you too! But don't try anything!" Adams swung around to look at Ben with a scowl but just as quick, he changed his expression back to one of sorrow.

"Of course!" he sobbed, "What can I do in comparison to everything that is going on out there!"

"What do you mean?" asked Charles.

"You know?.......Martial law and all that!"

Everyone looked at each other. Charles questioned,

"Martial law?" In this country?

"Yes, didn't you know? Adams continued gaining strength and excitement by the minute now the attention was on what he had to say. "It looks like they're finally going to push through this 'New World Order', that the conspiracy theorists used to constantly rant about. Ever since the disasters the Army seems to be in control of everything!" Lisa interrupted, changing the subject and calming the whole situation,

"Well you are safe here, Mr Adams. No-one will harm you now. Sam, would you take Mr Adams and go and see if there's a room anywhere?" Sam led Adams out of the room and down the corridor. Lisa turned to Jenny and Charles closed the door.

She said, "Jenny, could you ask Sharon if she would keep an eye on him. We can't trust this man, He will betray us!"

"Good move!" replied Jenny and ran off to find Sharon.

"How did he ever find this place?" Ben asked. "People knew of the House and Farm but not the new Ark! Something doesn't seem right about that man."

Lisa continued, "I know but let's just carry on and keep a close eye on him." Everyone began to leave.

"Charles, can we pray together?" she asked stopping him from leaving the room.

She closed the door and kissed him passionately. A surprised Charles took a breath and asked,

"What was that for? Not that I mind!" She replied,

"For being my hero, Charles! I love you so much!"

"I love you too!" he replied. They kissed again. "Now did you want me to pray with you or not?"

"Yes please, Mr Michaels!" she said, "Just so we're sure that we are 'singing from the same hymn book'!"

"I don't think there's a problem there, but yes of course!" Charles replied laughing.

*

The cavern looked fuller than ever but still felt relatively empty; it was such a huge area. There was a buzz about the place; people were excited to be alive and the presence of God truly filled every 'nook and cranny' there.

It was so exciting for everyone to see the prophecies from the bible coming to pass and living them out. Scripture tells us all that God does nothing without revealing it to the prophets first and so God's spirit, the Holy One of Israel, the Holy Spirit was right there in every decision that was being made, in every teaching that was heard and every step that was taken.

The parables of old were being unfolded and prophecies fulfilled right before their very eyes. To understand that the book of Revelation written all those years ago by the one who Yahshua loved was being lived and experienced, was mind blowing even if sometimes difficult to comprehend.

What was certain though, was that He as always, was reigning supreme, He was Sovereign overall, and they were seeing His purpose being fulfilled before their eyes. Everyone knew that the mouth of Yahweh had spoken and that His words would not return to Him void.

Chapter Five

Dissent in the Camp

In the days ahead, Charles and Lisa sat down and talked with the families that had recently joined them to give them a brief testimony of how they had been given the Ark by Old Mr Carter and where things were now after meeting Yahshua.

For many people the events that had unfolded had taken them by surprise and they now felt an urgency to make sure that their lives were pleasing to God. Studying the bible became a significant part of everyone's day.

The ancient ways of the scriptures were being brought back to life in believer's hearts, minds and deeds, just how Yahweh had always intended. The work of the Holy Spirit helped people to realise so many truths from the bible that had somehow been lost in modern explanations. Parables that Yahshua had taught two thousand years ago were understood in a whole new way and with a relevance to the times they were living in and the days that were ahead. People were developing a whole new lifestyle as they asked for His Word to be put on their hearts. Many people asked to be baptised again as their faith reached new levels of understanding. Testimonies were regularly given as part of the evidence of how God was working on them from the inside.

Christopher Adams seemed to integrate into life at the Ark pretty easily. As far as they all knew he had done nothing untoward and had actually helped out at some of the baptisms. He seemed to be a model citizen, the same as everyone else there and although Sharon still kept an eye on him. He was given the freedom that everyone else enjoyed there but having said all that, Lisa found it hard to trust him and she always kept in mind what Yahweh had said to her when he first arrived at the Ark.

Living underground was very different and the lack of natural light and fresh air made it critical to go outdoors as much as possible. Everyone took regular exercise as and when they needed it, although groups were kept to small numbers and sometimes even in the hours of darkness because hundreds of people standing on a mountainside doing push ups and star jumps would have raised suspicion to any kind of aircraft flying overhead. Since the disasters it was obvious that they needed to remain hidden as their 'practices' at the Ark were sure to be totally against what this 'New World Order' would be teaching and implementing. There had become a noticeable increase in military activity in the skies above them, so it made sense to keep their heads down. Christopher Adams had confirmed some of their fears with his talk of martial law and although Lisa wanted everyone to focus on the things of God and what the Holy Spirit was doing, she knew that it was important to keep abreast of what the enemy was up to.

*

One day, Lisa and Charles were in Ezra's room delving through the old books there, trying to uncover more 'gems' about this miracle called the Ark, when Lisa came upon a small leather-bound notebook similar to that of Old Mr. Carter's except it was slightly more battered and dog eared. It had obviously been well used.

"Could this be another book of great wonders!" She thought to herself and opened it with great anticipation to find the writings from Ezra, the weeping prophet. She looked at the book and flicked through the pages. At the very back of the book, at the bottom of the inside cover, she noticed a few words had been scrawled down in ink in a very neat hand. It said three words....

"For You, Lisa"

Lisa was thrilled and amazed. How could he know that she was coming? Just as Old Mr Carter had known. What faith they had. What a great God they served!

She sat down in the armchair to read her newly discovered treasure when the familiar small voice spoke to her,

"Stand at the crossroads," He said, "and ask for the ancient paths. Ask where the good way is and walk in it! There you will find rest for your soul!" Then nothing.

"Thank you, Father." replied Lisa and bowed her head, "Jeremiah, chapter six verse sixteen! You gave us that when we found this place, thank you!" He said nothing more which puzzled Lisa because whenever He had repeated things in the past it had always been because she hadn't properly understood what He was trying to tell her or that there was more to what He had said than had been first given.

"Stand at the crossroads and look?" asked Charles nonchalantly while jotting notes in the journal.

"Yes!" replied Lisa, "Again!" Charles smiled and put his pen down.

"I've had the same too!" he said.

"What do you think He's trying to say to us?" Lisa asked.

"I'm not sure," replied Charles, "but I know when He persists like this, I've usually missed something!"

Lisa laughed and smiled at him,

"Oh yes! I've found that too! So, why doesn't He just tell us?!"

"Because," replied Charles, "it's the search that develops our character into what it needs to be, to be who we need to be, to see His will being done on earth! It's critical, especially in these times!"

"I know, I know!" laughed Lisa, "And I know I need to deal with my impatience, it's just that I've never been very good at riddles and this feels like one!" Charles laughed with her,

"Well maybe that's it! Maybe you need to get good at solving them! This must be important for Him to repeat Himself and to give it to both of us! We must be missing something!"

Lisa agreed. She knew that study was a key factor in their time at the Ark but quite how much she had no idea. They both needed to put on their 'Indiana Jones' hats and get delving into scripture. She knew that in that room; the room where they found Ezra; the room where the fire never went out; there were secrets waiting to be found and truths that needed to be uncovered. She looked around at her surroundings; it fascinated her to think of the years of study that must have gone on in there and the mysteries of God that were sitting there waiting to be revealed.

"Let's pray before we begin." interrupted Charles, "We need all the help we can get!" Lisa agreed, and Charles prayed,

"Father Yahweh, maker of all that is good, we bless and praise Your Holy Name. We come to You in the Name of Your Son, Yahshua and ask You, by Your Holy Spirit, to guide us, teach us and reveal your heart to us. We ask You to put Your Word on our hearts, so we may know the truth. We give You all the glory, Amen."

"Amen!" replied Lisa enthusiastically, "Let's go!"

They felt like the more they learned the more they realised how little they knew and the more that needed to be discovered. The teachings they had both received in the past at Church seemed to have only skimmed the surface and didn't really give them the understanding that they now needed.

There was a knock at the door. Lisa jumped up to answer it to see Sharon with a troubled look on her face.

"I'm sorry to interrupt you guys!" She said,

"but I think you should come and see this! It's Mr Adams!"

Needing to hear no more, they rushed out of the room into the corridor toward the cavern to see what he was up to. When they reached the main cavern, they saw Christopher Adams standing on a rock, surrounded by a group of people and he was in full flow preacher mode. His face was red and intense, and his arms gestured wildly to enforce his strongly spoken words. They stood at the back of the gathering and listened to his speech. The gist of his message was that God had given him a dream and that Yahshua had returned and was right now in Jerusalem. He was so certain that this was true because it fitted perfectly with scripture. He gave chapter and verse and was very convincing with his delivery. The crunch came when he said that it was necessary for all believers now to go to Him and fulfil the prophecies.

"God is calling us to go and go now!" He shouted.

For those who had already met Yahshua, it was easy to believe that he would come back, after all they had seen Him face to face and some people were nodding in agreement with what Adams was saying. Lisa and Charles and the others that had gathered listened intently. He paused from his sermon and mopped his brow. He asked,

"Are there any questions?" Hands flew up.

He pointed to one of the people with their hand raised, who asked,

"And why would God tell you this and not Lisa? We are here safe and alive because of her obedience to Him! Why you?" Others agreed. Adams replied,

"Good question! I wondered the same too!" Lisa listened with interest as he continued. "God of course will use anyone! Even a donkey if we know our bibles!" He laughed, as did others listening. "But seriously, I have been a 'man of the cloth' for as long as I can remember and have been blessed in building the most successful church in this area! God uses whoever necessary to get the job done! He used Lisa to get us all here and now I believe He's telling me to lead us all to Jesus or Yahshua as some of you prefer to call Him! He has returned and waits for us on His Holy Mountain as I speak. We must go! We must go now!"

Lisa's heart sank as she listened to Adams and his message. She knew that it would sound convincing to some, but she also knew it couldn't be right or else why hadn't Yahweh told her. The unthinkable crossed her mind; did Yahweh want that man to take over from here? It didn't make sense. They were learning so much and being directed in such an incredible way. There was no way this could be true. She longed for the time to be with Yahshua again, but this wasn't it.

"Surely not? Father?" She asked under her breath. She heard a small voice in her head say,

"Watch out that no-one deceives you! For many will come in my Name claiming, 'I am the Messiah' and will deceive many!" Lisa replied,

"But he's not claiming to be the Messiah?"

The voice answered,

"You misunderstand, Lisa! Yahshua said that they confess that He, 'Yahshua' is the Messiah and yet they will still deceive many! Think about it.... No-one would be deceived if Christopher Adams claimed to be the Messiah! When Yahshua returns everyone will know! I told you ahead of time.......heed My Word and pray that you'll be counted worthy to escape!"

"Thank you, Father!" Lisa replied and spoke out to the group in front of her.

"I have a question, Mr Adams! If I may?" The room fell silent and people turned to look at Lisa.

"Yes, Mrs Jeffreys?" asked Adams nonchalantly, back to his arrogant self.

"Mrs Michaels, please." replied Lisa with a smile.

"Oh yes, sorry! I knew you before you were divorced!" replied the 'pastor'. Lisa bit her tongue and decided not to get involved in a petty fight and just asked her question.

"Aren't we told that everyone will all see him coming on the clouds with great power and glory? We haven't seen that?" Adams replied with a smirk on his face,

"Oh, I'm sorry, I thought you had already seen Him, or doesn't that count? I suppose you want to see Him again?"

Some around him laughed and others stared at Lisa waiting for a response. She stared at Adams as he smiled arrogantly back at her. She knew he would have an answer for everything and that he would twist scripture in making sure he was right. That was his nature; he had always done that. She turned and started to walk away. Adams shouted after her,

"What's the matter Lisa? Has the cat got your tongue? Or is it that you know I am right!?"

Lisa stopped in her tracks. Charles could tell by the look on her face that her patience had just been pushed to the limit.

"Don't do it Lisa!" said Charles. Lisa, with her eyes now closed as she took a deep breath and held her index finger in the air as though to 'shush' Charles, turned around and walked back towards Adams.

"Did you just ask if I think that you are right?" she questioned in a frighteningly calm tone. "You are about to lead an entire group of people, into danger and possibly their death and you think that I think you are right! No, the cat does not have my tongue Mr Adams. I have tried to control my tongue, but I think that maybe it's time something is said to you!" Adams abruptly interrupted,

"You know what your problem is, Lisa?! Ever since you left the safety of your local church and removed yourself from the covering of my pastoral authority, you have found yourself in one chaotic event after another. Look, even your house fell down and now you're living in a cave! Your life is a mess! You should admit that you were wrong and come with me! You need my covering. You're at risk of facing the wrath of satan if you stay here!"

"What a good idea!" Lisa said with a smile while joyfully clapping her hands together in total sarcasm. Then, with an increasing tone of annoyance and a touch more sarcasm she continued,

"I should submit to and follow a 'pastor' who teaches me to break the commands of God! Then I will only have to face God's wrath! Good plan, Adams!!" The cavern echoed his name while the watchers looked on in silence.

Charles gently took hold of Lisa's hand and led her away.

"Lisa," he said, "I think it might be a good idea to go and take a breather before things get really heated! Let Adams go, and anyone who wants to follow him." He led her back to Ezra's room where she dropped into the armchair by the fire.

"That man!" She huffed, "What is he trying to achieve?!"

Charles replied,

"He's either completely deceived himself or he is working for the other side!"

"But what about the people?" Lisa asked, "What should we say to those who listen to him?"

"Nothing, Lisa!" Charles responded, "If they want to leave and follow that man, they can. The right thing to do is to pray for them. Father told you that this would happen; that Adams would betray us, as well as others!"

"I know you're right." replied Lisa, "I just love them all so much and feel like I've failed them!"

"You are such a good woman, Lisa! That's why I married you and love you so much! The way that you feel is how the Father feels whenever His children are led astray. Yahshua died for us to be saved, not to get deceived and fall away!" She nodded and sighed and put her head back in the bible to carry on studying, although it was hard to think of anything else other than what they had just witnessed. Charles looked back to his bible too but found himself in exactly the same predicament as Lisa and couldn't concentrate. Every time they both put their heads down to study, within a moment they were both mentally back in the cavern arguing with Adams.

"Somehow, I don't think that this is the right time to be studying God's word!" Charles said interrupting the silence.

Lisa agreed and they both closed their books for the day.

Suddenly, the door flung open and Sharon burst in. She had obviously been running as she was out of breath.

She cried,

"Lisa, he's leaving! Adams has got a bunch of people together and they're actually leaving!"

"We can't stop them Sharon!" Lisa insisted.

Sharon exclaimed,

"But that lovely man Simon and John his friend who used to be a policeman. They're going too! So many people that I have come to know! Why are they listening to that fool, Lisa?"

"I can't answer that for you Sharon," sympathised Lisa, "but one thing is for sure; we need to pray for them, that their eyes will be opened and that they will have the strength and faith to get through the tribulation that they will meet!"

They could hear the chaos going on outside in the passageway. Some people were trying to talk others out of going and those who had decided to leave were trying to convince others to follow.

"Please, close the door Sharon and sit down for a moment." Lisa asked politely, "I can't bear to hear those who are leaving, I can recognise voices outside." But before she could close it, they heard the slam of their giant door closing behind Adams and the group of dissidents following him, who were now going to have to brave the world and the evil that it was beholden to. Lisa wept. It was so sad to know that some of their friends had been deceived by that man, but Yahweh had told her that it would happen. Charles consoled her; hurting too as they sat in Ezra's room. They prayed for their friends and cried many more tears but realised that even though they were now fewer in number and had lost loved ones, at least the betrayal was over, and Christopher Adams was hopefully, finally out of their lives.

Chapter Six

The Vision: Past

The Ark soon got back to normal and the atmosphere was much lighter without the presence of Adams. The whole incident, although sad, had created a new solidarity amongst the people of the Ark.

Back in Ezra's room, with the fire burning brightly, Charles was playfully pushing Lisa's impatience buttons by once again reiterating why it was so important to study and explaining how it would help develop their characters by searching for the truth, knowing that his reminders would wind her up.

"I know, I know!" she said to Charles impatiently, who was at the end of the table sniggering at the fact that he had got to her a little. Watching his shoulders jiggling with laughter only made things worse and she took one of Mr Carters books and proceeded to playfully hit him over the head with it.

"Ow!" protested Charles, still laughing, "Books aren't meant for that!"

The second 'wallop' on Charles' head caused a piece of paper to fall from the book she had used as her chosen weapon It fell on the table in front of the two of them. Something was written on the paper that grabbed Lisa's attention to such an extent, that she was even blind to Charles picking up another book to defend himself and potentially go on the offensive. Lisa was mesmerised; Charles was still laughing. Only when he saw the seriousness of the expression on her face and the intensity of her stare did he stop joking about and put his weapon down.

"What have you found?" he asked getting from his chair and moving around the table to Lisa's side. She didn't reply at first; she just carried on reading. After a moment she said,

"Charles look at this! Read it with me." Charles stood up and looked over her shoulder to read the words written in ink in a beautiful script with her. They read out loud the words;

When you stand at the crossroads and look,

ask for the ancient path, ask for the good way

and walk in it.

There you will find rest for your souls......

There you will find a place called Eden.'

They looked at each other inquisitively and Charles was just going to ask about that last line when there was a knock at the door. Charles walked to the door. He opened it to see a middle-aged, bearded man dressed in a white robe. For some unexplained reason and without a thought, Charles just stood back from the door and gestured an invitation for the man to enter the room. Lisa put the piece of paper down on the table, rose from her chair and went over to them both without saying a word. The man said, looking at them in turn,

"Charles, Lisa. Follow me." Without a question they vacated the room and walked down the corridor towards the main cavern. The man went ahead, and Charles and Lisa walked behind him, side by side.

"Do you recognise him?" whispered Lisa. Charles whispered back,

"His face is familiar, but I can't put a name to it!"

"It's Ezra! A younger version!" said Lisa behind her hand.

"Oh, my word! So it is! How does that work?!" responded Charles, wanting to go and say hello and apologise for not recognising him in the first place, but then thinking better of it. He leaned over to Lisa and whispered,

"Where do you think we're going?"

"Just follow me!" replied Ezra, overhearing Charles, walking ahead, still looking forward, "All will become clear soon enough!"

They followed on obediently. As they entered the main cavern, Lisa said,

"Where is everyone?!" There wasn't a soul about other than the three of them. This time Ezra didn't answer; he just kept on walking. The cavern was usually a vibrant hub of activity; people teaching; others making things or cooking something. There was always something going on; but not today. It was eerily empty.

They walked through the main cavern, down by the waterfall where people were always washing something; either clothes or utensils or themselves; but not today. Only the sound of the water could be heard. On past the private rooms they went; still no-one to be seen. Lisa gave Charles a look of 'What is going on?' without saying anything; knowing that Ezra would hear. He stopped and turned around to face them.

"Do not be afraid!" he said to them in a calming voice, "The Father wants you to see something. Just follow!"

So, they walked on down the long corridor past the myriad of rooms to the dark tunnel that Charles, who had mapped out all of the caves, knew was a dead end.

"Oh, this doesn't go anywhere!" blurted out Charles. Immediately he realised how foolish his words were and kept quiet as the tunnel mysteriously carried on into the distance. Ezra said nothing and just continued to walk. The tunnel got so dark that they lost sight of Ezra in front of them; so dark that they couldn't even see each other. Lisa grabbed Charles' hand for a little bit of extra security as they continued on with their journey. They couldn't see their feet or anything. It was like being blind again, but they just kept walking. It felt so strange; almost as though they were walking in deep space. They couldn't even feel the ground beneath their feet.

Suddenly, ahead of them a light shone in the distance. As they got closer to the light and they began to see each other, they realised that they couldn't see Ezra. Charles was just about to say something when a voice came from behind them.

"Don't worry! I'm here!" It was Ezra, of course but how he'd got behind them through all that darkness was beyond their imagination.

"Keep going! Not far now!" He said in a gentle voice. As they approached the light, they could hear the beautiful sound of bird song. The closer they got to the light the louder the sound became.

"What is this?" asked Lisa, "Is this real?" Ezra said nothing, Charles said nothing and just stared at the light.

They reached the end of the tunnel and their eyes squinted as they adjusted from the complete darkness to the brightness ahead. They both gazed in wonder at the vista before them. The air was warm and inviting and totally fresh with an indescribable, almost spice-like fragrance; the sky was deep blue and cloudless; the sun shining brightly in the sky. Beautiful trees and plants were everywhere, and a wonderful green grass carpeted the whole scene. Mountains bordered the horizon like a frame on a perfect picture. It was absolute paradise. Birds were flying all around; their song reflecting a happiness not known in the world experienced by Charles and Lisa. Ezra stood behind the awestruck couple and put his hands on their shoulders as they took in the beauty of this place before them.

"Welcome to Eden!" he said in their ears. "Shall we take a walk?!" Charles and Lisa looked at each other in total amazement. They smiled as their hearts were filled with a peace that they neither of them had ever witnessed before. They went to step onto the grass and Ezra pulled them back.

"Take off your shoes!" he said firmly, "This is Holy ground!" They apologised and slipped off their footwear.

"Sorry, Ezra!"

"Oh, you know who I am then?" he replied and led them onto the grass.

"Of course!" said Charles, "And, if you don't mind me saying, you're looking very well for your age!" They laughed and walked together, the beautiful grass between their toes.

"Ask any questions you wish as we walk." offered Ezra, "Otherwise I'll be quiet."

"I have one now, if that's okay?" Lisa enquired.

"Ask away!" replied Ezra. She asked,

"Are we dreaming or is this a vision?" Ezra smiled and said,

"Neither! This place is real, Lisa. It's just in the spirit world, a different realm, but you are alive and well here."

Both Lisa and Charles looked at him a little confused. He explained,

"I know it's hard to understand where you are but just relax and take in what Yahweh has for you here. He only ever does anything for the benefit of the person it is meant for and trust me, this is for you two."

They continued to walk around the 'garden' with Ezra following on a few steps behind, answering their many questions. They passed through meadows where they saw rabbits playing with foxes and lions and tigers and all kinds of animals they would have decidedly called wild, roaming freely and living very happily together. It was truly amazing. At one point, they were confronted with a mountain lion that wandered up to them and rubbed its face against Lisa's leg and purred exactly in the way that a domestic cat would have. Incredibly, she didn't even feel fear as the lion approached her; fear didn't belong in this place.

They saw a snake with legs, which provoked many questions which Ezra handled nonchalantly;

"Nothing in Eden crawls on its belly!" he answered. They were witnessing this place exactly how it was before the fall of man. Creation in perfection. Charles began to ask,

"So, are Adam and....", when something amazing began to take place which grabbed the attention of Ezra and all the animals and plants around them. They suddenly, dramatically became aware of an awesome presence; a tangible force that could be felt physically; an invisible force so strong it became impossible to stand up. Charles and Lisa sat down while Ezra got on his knees.

"What's happening?" asked Lisa. Ezra looked at her, smiled and said,

"It's love, Lisa! Pure love!" They soon followed suit and got on their knees. They realised what was happening; they were in the presence of the Almighty Elohim.

Wave upon wave of love came flooding towards them causing them to breathe deeply; almost gasping, taking it deep inside their bodies. Over towards a small group of trees they could see the source of the energy being emitted. There were two people walking in the trees. One of them, Lisa and Charles instantly recognised; it was Yahshua.

"Yahshua is here in Eden?" Lisa asked Ezra who nodded in response. She added, "Who is the other man?"

Ezra replied under his breath,

"It's Adam! The first Adam! We are back at the time when he tends the garden, and all is well."

Every living thing around them bowed as the King and his creation walked by. As well as Ezra, Charles and Lisa; all the animals took up a position of surrender and reverence. Even the plants and trees bowed in His direction. The love emitted by Yahshua was almost unbearable. It was an indescribable feeling of complete, overwhelming love and acceptance, mixed with infinite power and majesty. As they came out of the trees it was obvious that Yahshua and Adam were coming towards them. The three of them knelt on the ground.

"Hello Lisa, Charles!" came a voice they recognised as Yahshua's. They both tried to lift their heads and speak to Him but they were unable to; The power of His love was so great. Tears were streaming down both their faces. Neither had ever felt such power of emotion; almost too much for their human bodies to bear. As Yahshua walked past, Lisa lifted her eyes as much as she could and noticed His hands and feet were scarred which provoked an immediate question in her head, but she was unable and had no desire to speak any words. Instantly a voice said in her head,

"He is the Lamb who was slain from the creation of the world. "Amen!" She whispered, "Amen!"

Yahshua and Adam continued to walk through the woods and fields. The further they walked away from Charles and Lisa the more they found they were able to move until eventually they were able to lift their heads and stand.

"Wow!" said Charles.

"Wow! Lisa replied as they looked at each other. They hugged and thanked Ezra for enabling them to witness what they had.

"There is a lot more to come, children of the living God, a lot more!" Ezra replied. "Do you have any more questions?"   Lisa took a deep breath and said,

"Well, let me just get this straight.... Why I ask is because I noticed Yahshua's scars, which kind of messed with my head a little but then I had the answer given to me that He is the Lamb who was slain from the creation of the world. So that answered the question why His hands and feet are scarred here in Eden but then because Adam is here with Him messed with my head again and made me wonder, even though I realise that there is no such thing as time with God but......yes anyway!" She smiled; Charles and Ezra looked at each other and shrugged their shoulders.

Suddenly, their eyes were drawn to a beautiful fruit tree in the middle of the garden. Underneath the branches of the tree was a woman who seemed to be talking with one of those snakes with legs. It suddenly dawned on Charles and Lisa what was happening. They were about to witness the greatest tragedy in history, recorded in Genesis chapter two. The sorrow and horror of what was unfolding before their very eyes was unbearable. The woman looked up at the tree and put her hand up to reach for one of the fruits from the tree.

"No! It can't be!" screamed Lisa. "Don't do it!" Ezra held her back from trying to intervene.

"It has to happen, sweet child!" He said holding her arm tightly.

The next second, they heard the crunch of the fruit as the woman took a bite from it. The whole of creation fell silent and a cold darkness began to flow through Eden. From the fields Adam came running past Charles and Lisa, towards the woman. They seemed to argue with one another, then they both ran into the woods. The silence was eerie. Moments later they could see Yahshua walking in the woods, looking for Adam and calling his name. Again, they could feel the power emanating from Him. They knelt once more but were able to witness what was happening. They saw Yahshua talking with Adam and the woman then He turned and walked away. As He walked closer to where Charles, Lisa and Ezra were kneeling, the love grew stronger, but they could tell He was grieved. He walked over to them and laid His hands on Charles and Lisa's heads. They looked up at Him and into those beautiful eyes to see them filled with sadness; a teardrop formed and rolled down his cheek. As the teardrop hit the ground the sky turned black and rain clouds covered the Sun. Lightening flashed and thunder roared, a mighty wind blew, and rain lashed down on them all. The roar of a lion could be heard, followed by the cry of a deer as the lion killed his prey. Death had entered the world and already begun to take its cruel hold on the Fathers creation. They looked up as a giant angel descended from the sky and dragged Adam and the woman from the woods and pointed. They hung their heads and ran, closely followed by the angel. They ran past Charles, Lisa and Ezra and headed towards the dark tunnel where they had entered Eden. As Adam and the woman Eve entered the tunnel the angel stood on guard to ensure they didn't try to get back in.

Yahshua had gone. Charles, Lisa and Ezra all stood up.

"Come on! We had better get out of here!" shouted Ezra above the noise of the storm and they ran towards the angel and the tunnel home. As they approached the tunnel they could see the angel in more detail. He was awesome. He looked huge and carried a mighty presence himself. He held a massive sword in his hands, out of the scabbard, ready to use if necessary. Ezra led the way and they stepped into the tunnel back towards the Ark. Lisa was just about to ask Ezra another question when they heard the sound of someone crying. Ahead of them they could see two figures; it was Adam and Eve. She was sitting on the floor with her head in her hands, crying profusely. Charles and Lisa stopped as they drew nearer to them and Lisa tried to put her hand on the woman's shoulder in sympathy, but her hand passed through Eve. They were in different realms. Eve looked up at Adam, her face soaked in tears of remorse and cried,

"Take me back, please!" Then they disappeared into thin air.

Ezra hurriedly dragged Charles and Lisa away; it was time to leave.

"Let's go!" he cried, "This is not the place for us right now!"

Behind them they could see that the rain had stopped, and the clouds had dispersed. The Sun was shining, and all was well again in Eden, apart from the fact that man was no longer there, nor would he be again, until the plan of Yahweh was complete.

Chapter Seven

The Vision: Present

Throughout most of her lifetime Lisa had heard someone, somewhere complain about the fall and how Adam and Eve, particularly Eve, had let everyone in the human race down. She had heard people say that if she hadn't taken a bite from the fruit from the tree of knowledge of good and evil, we would have still been living in Eden and if Adam had been the man he was supposed to be, he wouldn't have left her alone to be tempted by the serpent and the consequential bite and it was to Adam that the command was given. Now Lisa had met Adam and Eve and seen their brokenness and their contrite hearts she felt a little different towards them. She knew that they were just people, like everyone else, susceptible to temptation. Lisa had now seen and felt the love that God has for His children, His companions and how broken He was when they chose to sin and disobey Him.

"Can I ask you a question, Ezra?" Lisa asked. He answered,

"Yes of course,"

"Okay," she paused then asked, "Why was it that after sin in Eden, we saw such an immense and immediate change but for thousands of years, millions of people have sinned every day and the world just carries on as normal?"

"Good question, Lisa!" Ezra replied, He stopped for a moment and closed his eyes as if to check and deliberate his answer. Then he continued,

"Eden is perfect, Lisa; it is paradise! So, the very second that sin entered in, it was dramatically obvious, and all creation mourned at that very moment. We don't notice the dramatic effect that sin has on the lives of people anymore because we are born into it and the world is now filled with it. But what you saw in Eden is the real effect of sin.

Many people assume that the anti-Christ appears during the times of the end, but he has been there from the beginning, deceiving God's children, causing them to doubt the words of the Most High. It's his most despicable deception, stripping the church of her power; of her life. However, do not be discouraged, as you have seen in times past when revival came, thousands returned to the ancient paths and opened their hearts to His Spirit. They combined their obedience with faith, just like Abraham did, and the kingdom of darkness suffered. Soon, once again there will come a great awakening, the dry bones are already rattling, when they arise their awakening will be unlike any other, for this awakening will not cease after a season, but will usher in the return of The King of Kings!

"Good answer! Thank you!" She replied, not fully able to process all that Ezra had said but knowing deep inside that there were many things that they had to learn.

As amazing as it was to be there in Eden, they were eager to return to the Ark; to be able to tell people about what they had witnessed. Ezra led the way and Charles and Lisa followed, chatting away, not paying any attention to where they were going.

They turned a corner and again they could see a light at the end of the tunnel but as they got closer to the light they noticed that instead of being back at the Ark, they were in open fields. As they walked into the daylight, they found themselves going over the brow of a hill. There were thick forests to either side. They stopped on the top of the hill and looked at the view ahead of them.

"Where are we?" asked Charles. Ezra replied,

"We are looking over the city of South Monhampton or New Hampton as it is now known. It's about a day and a half walk from the Ark."

"Yes, I know it!" said Charles, "I've been there several times in the past!" Lisa shrugged her shoulders; she'd never really left Wales much, only a few times on journeys with her parents as a child.

As they gazed over the city, it was a hive of activity; massive bulldozers were moving huge piles of rubble and twisted metal from demolished buildings caused by the devastation of the earthquake and at the same time there were new buildings going up everywhere. Cranes dominated the skyline, looking like enormous aliens, swinging huge pieces of steel into position. One thing was for sure, they were certainly re-investing in the place. Ezra continued,

"This is happening all over the world. Cities that were destroyed by the earthquakes are being rebuilt to suit the New One World Order. Synagogues of Satan, disguised as beautiful churches and synagogues are being put up everywhere. Laws have been passed to insist on Sunday worship. A one world religion with no other religions being tolerated. This is in an effort to put an end to wars and stop all the fighting, in the name of Peace!" Ezra turned to look at them both intently and said,

"This is only the beginning of the great deception and there is much yet to come and many will be deceived at that time. The anti-Christ will soon appear and will seem to bring peace and fulfil the nature and role of 'The Messiah', even establishing himself in

Jerusalem." He paused; obviously deeply moved by the words coming from his mouth and the pain caused by their manifestation. He continued,

"Our job is to prepare those who believe! Many who put up a fight will die; others will be kept safe but all who resist, whether they live, or die will ultimately have victory and spend eternity with Him. Ezra pointed. Charles and Lisa looked in the direction of his finger. They did a double take. Below them, they could see a group of people running across a field on the edge of the city. To their dismay they realised who it was they were watching. It was Christopher Adams and the people from the Ark. Ezra continued,

"Let's take a closer look!" Within a blink of an eye they 'zoomed in' and were standing watching the whole scene as though they were watching a movie on super widescreen television. They could see the group clearly, which saddened them, as they recognised the faces of those who had left; dear friends that they had spent much time with. They could also see a group of Border Policemen who were hiding watching Adams and his followers, waiting to ambush them.

Ezra narrated as they watched; "They are about to be arrested by the policemen you can see in front of them. They do not realise that with martial law, that has now been implemented and they are lawbreakers."

"For goodness sake! Stop them!" cried Charles.

"We can't!" insisted Ezra, "We are not there! We are here!"

"Isn't that the same place?!" questioned Charles desperately.

"No!" demanded Ezra, "We and they exist in two different realms!"

Sure enough, the police jumped out and herded the group together, shouting and pointing their automatic guns at them.

They watched on as Adams and the group were bundled into the back of a Police vehicle, all apart from two men.

"Look! There's Simon Johnson and John Fisher, his friend the ex-policeman talking with that officer.

"So, is this happening now?" Lisa asked Ezra who smiled and said,

"Oh yes! This is as live as it can get!"

"So how did you know that was going to happen?" asked Charles.

"Because Yahweh told me!"

They watched on as Simon and John were suddenly pushed to the ground and hand-cuffed behind their backs. Then they were pulled back to their feet and dragged to the vehicle to join the others.

Ezra entered into narrator mode once more;

"They will be taken into custody and questioned. Then they will be put through a screening process and introduced to a certain 'Sister Mary Jane', who sounds harmless but is far from it. She is an agent for the enemy, for the New World Order. Most of them will fail the screening process and be sent to a camp for rehabilitation, which is where we're going to go now!"

"Most of them?" asked Lisa.

"Yes, most of them!" Ezra replied, "Only Adams will pass!"

They blinked and the scene in front of them changed and they found themselves sat on a grassy bank in front of what looked like a concentration camp of World War Two. Ezra continued,

"We need to observe what happens next and learn. Remember we are in the spirit realm and cannot affect the outcome. That is in Yahweh's hands! But you can pray and petition on their behalf. The truth is though, Yahweh knows what's best and what needs to happen for their benefit."

Two buses pulled up at the gates of the camp and were duly allowed to enter. They could see the doors of the buses open and what can only be described as 'inmates' were allowed off. This included John, Simon, the others from the Ark and a bunch of strangers.

"So, is this happening now?" asked Charles, to which Ezra replied,

"Yes, they were in the police station overnight, but this is now." He smiled nonchalantly and looked back towards the camp. Charles was slightly confused. He leant over to Lisa and said,

"So now is today which is the day after yesterday which is also now?" Lisa replied,

"Sounds good to me!"

Charles asked Ezra,

"Who are the strangers?" He replied,

"They are others who haven't submitted to the terms of the New World Order."

"And what are the terms?" asked Lisa. Ezra replied,

"You will see."

The captives all went into a room, where a video of wars and atrocities was playing on a large screen. They saw pictures of the holocaust and other gruesome scenes being labelled, "All done in the name of religion." The video finished, and a uniformed man got up to give a talk about the new way of living that their government was providing for them all.

"All you will need to do," he said, "is to sign a declaration stating the acknowledgement of your rejection of the old biblical laws given to Moses, which bring curses and death, and embrace the laws of the New World Order which bring life, equality and peace! That is all you need to do, and you will be on the next bus home!"

"Don't believe it!" cried one on the inmates who was duly overpowered by the man raising his voice. He continued,

"You will be given a substantial amount of money to build a new life for yourselves and your families. Those who want to do this now…," the man paused, picking up a card to read, "…. just raise your hand and one of our team will take you out and pray with you, sign the declaration and that will be it. You will be back with your loved ones tomorrow at the latest. The rest of you will be kept here in the camp until you see sense. It's as simple as that, ladies and gentlemen!"

About fifty percent of the room immediately raised their hands and were ushered out of the room. They were congratulated and sat down at tables, where they gave their lives in prayer to the 'god of light'. As they signed the declaration a heaviness came over Lisa and Charles and they were immediately taken back in their minds to Eden and everything they witnessed with Adam and Eve. A sticker similar to a nicotine patch was put on their right hands or their foreheads; the choice was theirs. They were then escorted from the building, presumably to return home.

John, Simon and most of those from the Ark stayed in their seats. Some held their head in their hands; it was a horrible situation to be in but they resisted. The captives were then taken to accommodation huts in the centre of the camp, which were dank and dreary just how you would imagine things to be in a prison.

Ezra continued,

"They're going to suffer this for the next six weeks; films, talks, beatings, chances to be back with loved ones. They will be given very little food and be made to work hard for what they do get. What you will see from now on is their final hours! Watch!"

The scene switched again. They watched John being woken abruptly by one of the guards thumping on the door of his hut and shouting his number along with a few others. He got dressed quickly and met the guard outside. The guard told them,

"You have to go to a counselling session, this morning! You've been here for six weeks now! Come on! Follow me!"

John followed, with three other inmates who had been with him since they had first arrived. Across the camp they could see other inmates from other huts being led in the same direction towards the main centre area. They all converged on a small conference room and were told to go in and find a seat. Simon was in one of the queues to go in, his shoulders seemed to be hunched over in an almost defeated gate. He was badly bruised. John smiled at him and gave him a wink to say 'everything will be okay' but Simon hardly acknowledged him. The look on Simon's face concerned John. There was about fifty or so people in the room that was filled with an atmosphere of dread. A heavy presence of armed guards surrounded the doorway and the corridor to the room. When everyone was sat down, and the guards came in and began strapping people's legs to their chairs with cable ties. A couple of men struggled against them only to receive a blow on their heads from the guard's truncheons. Blinds were pulled down over the windows and the lights were switched off, leaving them all in complete darkness, fastened to their chairs.

There was a daunting, sinister feel in the room. John remained calm, but all the others shouted and screamed out loud. In a strong voice John spoke out in prayer amidst the chaos.

"Heavenly Father," he cried, "You are the mighty one, the Holy one, the Most High God and maker of heaven and earth. We thank you for giving us the strength to have held out for this long, but Father I ask you for more now, right now!" He paused for a second. The room had fallen silent. He continued, "Fill us with your Spirit, Father and give us the power we need to hold out and get through this time. Help us to resist and to wait for you! Come Holy Spirit, rescue us all from this prison. In the name of Yahshua Jesus Christ Amen!"

An echo of "Amens" resounded, only to be cut short by the door suddenly bursting open and the bright fluorescent lights switched on. Everybody squinted their eyes with the sudden change from darkness to light, as the petite figure of the infamous Sister Mary Jane strode into the room with a guard by her side. She stood and glared menacingly at everyone there. She was wearing a black fitted suit and a nun's veil along with bright red lipstick. She stood at the front with her hands on her hips and snapped,

"We have given you so many chances to conform to god's new way of living! You have had so many opportunities to give your life to the new order of things and to the god of light and yet you still refuse to listen to see sense!" She paced around still keeping her hands on her hips. She stared at the inmates one by one and continued in a calmer voice,

"We have come to the end, ladies and gentlemen!" There was silence. "Give your lives today or we will have to deal with you in a very different way!" The guard 'cocked' his machine gun; Sister Mary glared and said,

"Raise your right hand to choose life or otherwise keep your hands down."

There was no movement for a few seconds and then a woman at the front lifted her hand, followed by two more men. Then more and more people lifted their hands, including many from the Ark, to the complaint of those who were resisting. John kept his tight by his side.

"My God! Rescue me!" he said to himself as he gripped his chair. Simon was sat somewhere behind John, so he could not see how he was coping, as more and more raised their hands. Mary Jane shouted,

"Guards free those who have chosen life! Well done everyone, you know it makes sense! Praise the god of light!" The guards rushed to the chairs and released those who had succumbed to the threatening call of the enemy and they wandered to the exit door leaving John and the remnant who had held on in their seats. John was visibly distressed as he saw friends from the Ark leaving and that one of the men walking towards the door was Simon.

"Guys!" He shouted and was immediately belted by a guard, on the back of his head. Simon looked back at John. The expression on his face said "sorry" and "thank you" at the same time. John wept. He couldn't believe it; Simon and his other friends had held on all this time and given in right at the end. Everyone passing through the door was congratulated and given a round of applause by the people in the corridor, apart from Sister Mary Jane who continued to scowl at those left in their seats. She stared directly at John and the corners of her mouth turned up to smile an almost victorious smile. The door was closed behind them and the remnant was left in the room still strapped to their chairs to ponder on their fate. The hubbub of celebration continued outside as John looked around to see who was left. It was a handful. Twelve to be exact including himself.

"Stick with it, guys!" John exclaimed, "Just believe!"

Suddenly, from the celebrations outside, came a shout from one of the guards,

"Stop! You! Stop or we'll shoot!" The next thing they heard was a single shot of a gun which seemed to echo all over the countryside, followed by people crying out at the scene they had just witnessed. Someone had tried to escape, and they had shot him down like a rabbit. John tried to stand up with the chair strapped to his leg and strain to look out of the window but couldn't. They left the remnant of believers in their chairs while the ceremonial altar call took place and the people dedicated their lives to the god of light and pledged allegiance to the New World Order. John used the time to talk to the eleven others that were left, about Yahweh. He told them all about Yahshua's visitation to the Ark and his promises he made to them.

"What is the alternative anyway?" he said, "To live a life marked by the beast? I would rather die!" Everyone agreed.

Charles and Lisa sat amazed.

"Wow! What a leader he is!" exclaimed Charles. Lisa had to agree. She said,

"I never knew he had such faith!"

They left John and the eleven fastened to their chairs all night and were given nothing to eat or drink. Some tipped their seats over on one side to get some kind of sleep before the following morning, when they were finally released from their chairs.

After sunrise, the guards burst into the room and the cable ties were snipped and the prisoners were pulled to their feet. They were bound with their hands behind their backs and pushed outside into the sunshine, where they were surprisingly faced with an enormous, silent crowd of inmates, with a row of heavily armed guards keeping them back.

John and the other eleven, were pushed and shoved around by the guards who were enjoying every minute as they took them across the field. They walked past a dead body lying on the grass. It was Simon; He had been the one that had been shot trying to escape. His body was left there to rot as a reminder to the rest of the inmates not to try and escape. John looked at Simon's bloody, fly swarmed carcase for a second and thanked God that he was now with Him, before being pushed forward by the butt of a rifle in the small of his back, so hard that he almost fell. The guards were laughing and taunting them, as they rounded the corner of a building and were led to the main square with the throng of inmates following on.

Charles and Lisa saw the look of despair on John's face as he looked at the sight before his eyes. In the middle of the square, where the flag of the NWO was flying, was a row of twelve guillotines. Some screamed and almost fainted as they were dragged by the guards towards the square.

John shouted to the others,

"Hold it together, everyone! Trust in Yahweh! Keep the faith!" The guards laughed and mocked them all the more. John was kicked in the back in his knees which made him fall to the floor. Some guards turned on John for shouting out and kicked him while he was on the ground. One guard screamed at him,

"Shut it! Jesus freak!" and kicked him in the face. Then they dragged him by the hair into the middle of the square and dropped him like a sack of potatoes. They lined up the twelve, in front of their appointed guillotine and the crowd was ushered closer by the guards, to witness the proceedings.

"We can't just let this happen!" objected Lisa. Ezra said nothing but just kept watching.

A voice came over the public-address system. It was Sister Mary Jane on a platform next to the place of execution. She spoke out,

"These people are traitors and will be made an example of! They have refused to conform to the new covenant between our god of light and the world. They will not reject the laws of their bible, a book that is old and outdated, filled with ridiculous and harsh rules which today's masses could never live by. So today, they will die, and you will all watch them. Meditate on what you see! Learn from this experience and give yourselves over to the god of light and save yourselves from this! But before I call on the executioner, I am going to give these wretches one more chance." She turned to the twelve. "Will you renounce your God, His commandments and the so- called Messiah and accept the one true god of light into your lives and say that he is the only god in this world and embrace the ways of the One World Order as your new way of living?" All went quiet. Miraculously the twelve stayed silent. They looked at John who spoke quietly but with great strength,

"Hang tough! Have faith!" The rest maintained their silence.

"Very well then!" Sister Mary continued, "Executioner, do your duty!"

A short man wearing a black mask sat on a chair next to a box with a button on to release the blades. The twelve were shoved forward by the guards, to their guillotines. They were pushed to their knees and forced to put their necks on the plastic blocks. As they knelt there, John led them in prayer and all twelve spoke aloud in union as Sister Mary led a countdown;

"The Lord *is* my shepherd; I shall not want."

"Ten!"

"He makes me to lie down in green pastures;

"Nine!"

"He leads me beside the still waters. He restores my soul;

"Eight!"

"He leads me in the paths of righteousness For His name's sake."

"Seven!"

"Yea, though I walk through the valley of the shadow of death, I will fear no evil;

"Six!!"

"For You *are* with me; Your rod and Your staff, they comfort me."

"Five!"

"You prepare a table before me in the presence of my enemies;"

"Four!"

"You anoint my head with oil; My cup runs over."

"Three!"

"Surely goodness and mercy shall follow me"

"Two!"

"All the days of my life;"

"One!"

"And I will dwell in the house of Yahweh Forever!"

"Zero! Go!" she screamed.

"Amen!" the twelve cried.

"In Yahshua's name, Stop!" shouted Lisa.

The swish of the blades descending could be heard all around the camp. What happened next could only have ever been described by the twelve themselves. At first, they just looked at each other.

"Are we dead?" asked one of the twelve.

"I don't think so!" replied John as he got up off his knees. "Mind your heads when you get up! These blades are sharp you know!" One by one they got up off their knees and hugged one another, praising God as they did so.

Time was literally standing still. The blades had stopped about two feet above their heads. They could see the crowd; some gasping, others with their hands over their eyes, some just looking at their feet, but all absolutely stationary; frozen in time. They could see the executioner with his finger on the button and across on the platform was Sister Mary Jane passionately grimacing, a face intensely consumed with evil.

"Come on!" shouted John, "Let's get out of here!"

They jumped off the scaffold and were just about to run when one of the twelve, a man called Justin shouted,

"Hang on, there's something I have to do!" He jumped up onto Sister Mary Jane's platform and smudged her bright red lipstick right across her face to the cheer of John and the rest of the gang.

Then he took the pen out of her top pocket and wrote on the back of her hand;

'Yahweh was here!'

"Come on Justin!" shouted John, laughing with the rest of them, "Let's go! They might wake up!" With that they all ran like the wind, John leading the way. They dragged Simon's body out of the camp with them and headed for a group of trees where they made a grave for Simon's body by covering it with a pile of rocks to keep wild animals away. They prayed and thanked Yahweh for Simon and praised Him like never before. He had truly saved them.

They started to head for home, back to the Ark, walking toward the bank where Charles, Lisa and Ezra were sat. As they walked alongside them, Charles smiled and said,

"Well done, John!"

John looked at them and replied,

"Thank you!"

Chapter Eight

The Vision: Future

Charles and Lisa both gasped, completely taken aback, that John had answered them and could obviously see them too. Charles stood up immediately and went to shake his hand. Ezra held his arm back and whispered in his ear.

"Remember where you are, Charles!" He pulled his hand away and just looked at John face to face.

Their attention was quickly drawn back to the camp as a loud swish and thump of the guillotine blades hitting the blocks and a huge roar from the crowd of onlookers echoed through the hills.

In an instant, Charles, Lisa and Ezra were transported through time and back in a dark tunnel presumably in the Ark.

"Whoa!" cried Charles and Lisa simultaneously. Ezra smiled.

"So where are we now?" asked Lisa.

"We are carrying on our journey, please follow." replied Ezra who just turned and walked down the dark corridor. Charles and Lisa hurriedly followed on behind. Charles asked,

"So, what happened back there? How was it that John could see and hear us? I thought we were in the spirit realm and couldn't effect anything?" Ezra answered without turning around or stopping,

"When time was paused, there was a crossing over; a collision of realms. So even though you could see and talk to John, you weren't really there!"

"Oh right!" said Charles, "That's as clear as mud then!"

They all laughed and continued the walk down the corridor.

"Another question?" asked Lisa.

"Yes" replied Ezra. Lisa continued,

"Why did we need to see all that?" Ezra smiled and said,

"Well, you have now seen the reality of what is going on in the outside world and this is only the beginning. Ezra continued,

"You all need to learn how to avoid deception and the importance of listening to and being obedient to the words of The Most High! Most importantly you will have seen that the spirit of the anti-Christ is all about lawlessness. He deceives the children, causing them to doubt the eternal words of The Father."

"Yes! I saw that!" Lisa replied, and they continued on with their journey. Ezra continued "he who is yet to come in the name of the Messiah will quickly show his true nature, he is the man of lawlessness. For thousands of years the spirit of the anti-Christ has dressed his message in a message of 'love', leading the children of the Most High astray, causing them to fall into the error of lawlessness, but true love is defined in 'One John five verse three, obedience to the commands of the living God.

As they continued to walk a light could be seen ahead and Lisa and Charles knew that meant that there was more to come. They walked hurriedly with anticipation; their hearts beating faster in their chests as they came closer to the light. Something huge was coming up. They could feel it.

As they neared the end of the corridor they could hear birds again and feel the heat from a summer breeze. They stopped at the entrance to the outside and gazed across a wonderful landscape of hills, mountains and valleys, beautiful blue skies edged with rugged mountains on the horizon.

"This, dear Charles and Lisa, is the future." explained Ezra; tears in his eyes, "This is the safe place!" He stepped out onto the grass and Charles and Lisa followed.

"So, where are we now?" Lisa asked.

He smiled as he looked at their confused faces and said, "Come!"

They followed, looking all around, taking in all the sights and sounds. Fragrances of soft spices drifted by from time to time which heightened their senses. Along with the sound of the birds singing above them, they could also faintly hear what sounded like choirs of angels singing in the distance. As they walked, the singing got more and more pronounced and they could start to pick out some of the words that were being sung. They could hear the words, "Holy, Holy, Holy, Yahweh Most High, who was and is and forever will be!" being sung over and over. Ezra led them through a small group of trees and the sight that met them took their breath away.

They were standing on the top of a ridge, with the ground sweeping away from them; beneath them was a natural amphitheatre of colossal size. They were looking down on thousands upon thousands of people dressed in pure white, dazzling robes. There were too many to count or even guess the number. Even with all the football matches Charles had watched in his life, he couldn't begin to guess how many were in front of them. It had to be millions. They were all facing a large round area encircled by huge stone chairs and in the centre of the circle was another circle with a powerful bright, white light emitting from it. They walked down the grassy slope towards the immense throng. Standing at the back of the crowd were two people they instantly recognised. It was Adam and Eve looking radiant in their robes. Charles tried to say something, but no words could come out. As they stepped through the crowd, moving closer to the circle, they saw people they had known from the past, some family members they hadn't seen for years and even some famous people.

Neither of them could say a word but in reality, they were totally 'dumbstruck' anyway with the visions their eyes were witnessing. They came to a small clearing in the sea of people and stopped and stood in the middle of it. It was as though it was an area reserved for them. They turned around and looked at all the faces, none of which were looking at them; everyone's eyes were transfixed on the circle with the chairs. Lisa nudged Charles and pointed at someone. It was Jenny! In her robe! Behind her stood Ben too. As they looked around more they saw more people who right now should have been at the Ark. They saw Sam, Jim and Connie and all the gang that they had grown to love so much.

Suddenly, they both stopped turning around and stared at two people they both knew better than anyone else in the world. It was themselves! Charles and Lisa looked at each other then looked back at themselves stood there in a crowd of people, their eyes fixed on the light in the centre circle. Charles looked down at himself and patted his thighs to make sure he was still there and sure enough he was, in his scruffy old clothes. He went to walk over to himself, but Ezra stopped him. Ezra looked at him with a smile and said without moving his lips,

"You're not here, Charles! Remember?! At least the you in the now isn't!"

All at once, the choir stopped singing and the light that was emitting from the centre circle blasted out with such intensity you could almost hear it. It stretched all the way to the sky and was so bright that it created an immediate reaction to cover their faces, but they soon realised that despite its intensity they could still look at it. They could feel the power from it on their skin and yet it was as a glowing warmth rather than a harsh burn. A feeling of love, just the same as they had felt in Eden, came from the light and became too much to bear; so weighty that it was impossible to stay upright but instead of sitting down everyone instinctively got down on their knees and planted their faces in the grass. The trees around the 'arena' all bent towards the circle and all the animals there bowed down in submission. It was an incredible sight. Suddenly there was a huge shout, and everyone stood up and sang at the top of their voices,

"Salvation belongs to our God who sits on the throne! And to the Lamb!" They sang a melody that just flowed naturally from their bodies; a God created and ordained melody.

The chairs around the circle were now taken with elderly looking men, all with their eyes fixed on the immense light from which they could begin to make out the figure of another man. He stepped out of the light and stood before them all. The crowd cheered. His hair was white as snow and He wore a white robe that glistened with sparkling jewels like diamonds. It was the King of Kings, Yahshua! He looked so different to how they had seen Him before, but they knew it was Him. Light emitted from his eyes and mouth as he stood there with His arms stretched wide; a stance that someone would take when greeting a long-lost friend but also the stance He took when He allowed Himself to be hung on that cross at Calvary. Light could be seen blasting through holes in His hands, feet and side. It was an incredible sight filled with great power and majesty as well as brokenness and suffering. Everyone was in complete awe before the all-powerful King of the Universe. This was it, as Ezra had said. They were finally in the safe place.

Seven large men gathered around Yahshua, each with a trumpet in their hands. They turned and faced the crowd, who in turn fell silent. It was a silence that Charles and Lisa had never witnessed before. They could hear absolutely nothing. Yahshua stepped forward and all creation bowed their heads. Tears streamed down Yahshua's face as He beckoned one of the angels to His side. The light from the circle dimmed in intensity as the angel lifted a trumpet. The atmosphere became one of sadness and grief rather than the triumph they had just been witnessing a few moments before. The angel brought the trumpet to his mouth and gave a long blast. In a second, Charles and Lisa found themselves back in the dark corridor of the Ark.

Still awestruck, they followed Ezra down the dark corridor.

"So where are we going now?" asked Lisa feeling a little drained from the emotional roller coaster they'd been on that day.

"Oh, you know it well!" replied Ezra, "But just follow me, there are things that need to be seen!"

They turned a corner and saw a light ahead again and wondered where they were now and what glimpse Yahweh was going to give them this time. However, the closer they got to the opening the more they recognised the location they were being taken too. They stood at the entrance with Ezra and surveyed the main cavern back at the Ark. They were back home; at least their temporary home. This time it was full of people, but they were all 'frozen', all put on 'pause'. Ezra turned to Charles and Lisa,

"You've been given a glimpse today of the past, present and future." he said, "And as you reflect on what you have seen today and keep in mind the love of your Saviour. Remember in Eden how He wept for Adam and again in the future He weeps before His children reap what they have sown. There is much trouble in the world that Lucifer is causing but it is nothing compared to the wrath of God that will come upon the earth. Although the salvation you gain from giving your all to Yahshua may not save you from all tribulation, most importantly it will save you from Yahweh's wrath which is beyond anything the devil can cause. Believe me, sweet children of the Most High, the love that He has for you knows no boundaries and nothing will ever separate you from that. That love is for all and you two must emulate that love the best you can. You have felt the power of true love and now must do everything you can to help others to discover it for themselves. Look at these people in here, frozen in time. Look at their hearts as they are working away!" They looked around. A strange sensation came over them. Ezra continued,

"Each one was loved dearly by their mothers and fathers when they were children, but the way Yahweh sees them is with a love many times stronger, so much so, that He was willing give His Own Son for them, who willingly gave His own life on the cross at Calvary." Charles and Lisa began to weep. Ezra looked at them as they cried and said, "I have been instructed to pass this compassionate heart on to you, that sees and feels the pain of others as much as your own. Let's walk!"

They dodged around the people to get through to the other side of the cavern and walked up the corridor towards the room they first met their friend. He continued,

"Your calling is great, Charles, Lisa!" He looked at them in turn. "You have much to learn, truths to be revealed to you as to many others, truths which if applied will qualify you to be counted worthy to escape the troubles that are ahead. But just remember...." he said as he opened the door to his old room, ".... the things that you have seen!" They walked into the room and Jenny, Ben, Sophie, the boys, Sam, Jim and Connie were all 'frozen' in there. The only thing that was moving was the flickering flames of the fire.

The door closed behind them and Ezra was nowhere to be seen. Lisa placed her hands on the heads of her two dear boys and as she did they turned their heads and smiled lovingly at their mummy and in an instant the whole of the Ark 'thawed'.

"Mummy did you see the angels?" asked Josh

"Which angels, sweetheart?" Lisa questioned. Josh replied,

"The ones with big swords who were guarding you!" Lisa looked puzzled, she had seen many angels that day but none with large swords.

"It's true!" continued Jenny, I came in here about ten minutes ago and you were sat at the table here reading and there were seven angels in here surrounding you guys! We all stood here watching them, then they just disappeared into thin air!"

"So how long have we been gone?" asked Charles. Jenny replied,

"Gone? Gone where? You've been with us all the time!"

Chapter Nine

Back at the Ark

The news came.

"John and the others are back!"

Everyone dashed out of Ezra's room and into the corridor and down to the cavern where John and the gang were being welcomed by everyone. They looked thin and dirty; their clothes ragged and worn but their faces were glowing; overjoyed to be back at the Ark with their brothers and sisters. John saw Charles through the crowd and immediately ran to him to give him a hug.

"Wow man!" John whispered into his ear as they hugged, "It's so good to be back! I'm so sorry for leaving and not trusting you guys!"

"The important thing is that you're back and safe!" replied Charles fighting back the tears, "We love you all so much!" John squeezed a little tighter.

"Yahweh is so cool!" He said, "You should have seen what happened out there!"

"I know He is!" replied Charles, "And you are all real heroes! Now go and relax and get cleaned up and then come and tell everyone what happened!" replied Charles.

"What's wrong with now!" laughed John, "I'm a tough old boot you know!"

"I know you are!" replied Charles, "And I know more than you think!" John smiled and looked into his eyes. Charles' words triggered something in his mind that he couldn't quite remember.

"Yes, I believe you do, Charles" He stepped back with a puzzled expression on his face and smiled, "I believe you do!"

"Get cleaned up, get something to eat and have a rest!" Charles insisted, "Then you can all tell us about your adventure!" John agreed. He gathered the others and told them to do the same. The celebrations died down and the Ark returned to its normal, peaceful self.

"Oh, it's so good to have them back!" said Lisa, smiling as she held Charles' hands.

"It sure is!" replied Charles, "At least some of them anyway!" Their smiles dropped as they remembered the ones who had given in to the demands of Sister Mary and were now in a living hell, outside of the safety of Yahweh. The sorrow they felt for them was truly painful and both of them hugged as they wept on each other's shoulders.

"Yahweh said it would happen!" Lisa mumbled through the tears. Charles replied in the same manner,

"I know but they really were family! I loved them so much!" Lisa nodded; she couldn't talk anymore.

They took each other by the hand and walked back towards Ezra's room.

"I have something I need to tell you, Charles." said Lisa quietly as they walked slowly through the corridor, "But I can't right now, it will have to wait for a while." Charles stopped in his tracks.

"What?! You can't do that! Tell me!" he demanded.

"No, it's not the right time." she insisted.

"Lisa! Tell me!" Charles demanded again, bursting with curiosity.

"Not now Charles!" Lisa re-insisted. Their argument was interrupted by Jenny shouting them both,

"Charles, Lisa! John and the others are back, ready to tell their stories!" Lisa turned immediately heading back to the cavern, leaving Charles standing alone in his frustration. He followed them to the main room to be greeted by a clean fresh looking, John with a beaming smile.

"That was a quick sleep!" Charles laughed, forgetting his frustration with his wife.

"I couldn't sleep if I wanted too!" replied John. They both laughed.

"Come on! Gather around!" ordered Jenny, "Let's give these heroes a proper welcome back!" Everyone cheered, applauded and encircled John, Justin and the others as they began to relate the stories of the past six weeks. They heard about the New World Order and Sister Mary Jane and how they were treated in the camp. John told them about Simon and the struggle he had at the camp and his subsequent death at the hands of the guards. He told them,

"Yahweh has a special place for Simon, just as he does for all those who give their lives for His sake! As it says in Matthew five, 'for his is the kingdom of heaven'!" Everyone loved Simon at the Ark and it was sad to hear the story, but they were comforted knowing that they would see him again, unlike those whose souls had taken the mark. Each of the twelve gave testimony to the horror of the day of execution and the jubilation of their rescue. A real message of just who is in control came flooding out of the stories and the privileged place they hold by being at the Ark.   Justin retold his antics with Sister Mary Jane which brought delight to everyone.

"But we have to be on guard!" John stressed, "We have to be watchmen! The enemy wishes to devour us all, but no matter how hard he tries, he will fail! Yahweh already has the victory!" Everybody cheered.

Lisa nudged Charles and whispered in his ear,

"Hey, have you forgotten something?" Charles replied,

"No, what?" Lisa continued with a cheeky smile,

"I have something that I need to tell you!" Charles was immediately taken back to the argument before the testimonies began.

"Come on! We have to go!" he whispered back. He took hold of her hand, winked at her and said, "We've seen this before anyway!"

They stealthily snuck out of the cavern without being seen, so as not to detract from the storytelling. On their way up the corridor, Charles asked again,

"So, come on tell me!"

"Patience, patience! Mr Michaels!" Lisa laughed, "I would like some privacy, if you don't mind!"

They went back to their bedroom and Lisa sat on the edge of the makeshift bed.

"Come and sit here with me!" said Lisa patting the bed beside her. Charles sat down, a little concerned at the formality of Lisa's tone of voice. She smiled a broad grin and spoke the words that every husband longs to hear from his wife;

"Charles, I think I'm pregnant!" Within a second his emotions travelled from concern to surprise to pure ecstatic joy. He jumped up onto his feet and cried out,

"You're kidding me! Oh wow! Oh, Praise God! That's amazing!" Lisa put her finger up to her mouth for him to quieten down,

"Shush! Do you want everyone to know?!" she whispered.

"Well Yes!" Whispered Charles loudly, "Don't you?"

"We'll tell them soon!" replied Lisa, "I just wanted this to be between you and me for now!" They kissed and hugged each other passionately.

"I love you, Lisa!" said Charles softly. Lisa replied,

"And I love you too!" They kissed again.

"So, when can we tell everyone?" enquired Charles impatiently, "I can't keep this in for long! You know how bad I am at keeping secrets!" Lisa smiled at her dear husband and looked him lovingly in the eyes,

"We'll know when the time is right!"

*

The following morning, all the leaders met with John and the eleven who relayed the whole story to them in more detail. John began by apologising to everyone about them leaving the Ark in the first place.

"He just sounded so convincing and with him being a pastor and all." John reasoned. "But I for one am truly sorry and would ask you all to forgive us."

"Me too!" said Justin.

"And me!" said the next and all the eleven agreed.

"Listen," said Charles, "forgiveness isn't the issue here! Of course, we forgive you! We just were so sad when you left because we knew how clever Adams is and how feasible his argument sounded." He paused cutting a long story shorter, "We're just so happy to see you all back and as you said, Simon will be rewarded just as Yahshua said, as I believe we all will if we focus on Him and His ways!" Everyone agreed. John continued,

"I wish you could have been a fly on the wall and have seen everything!" Charles and Lisa just smiled at each other. Somehow right now didn't seem the right time to say that they had seen it all albeit in a different realm. This was John and the gang's testimony and right that they should explain all that they saw.

The main information that came out of the meeting was that there was truth in many of the so-called conspiracy theories that had been banded around prior to the belt of Orion exploding. Indeed, most of the eleven agreed that one of the scariest things of all was the admittance within the newly formed government of the N.W.O. that the population of the world needed to decrease considerably.

"They are happy to kill for the slightest reason!" Justin told them all. "And anyone stepping out of line with their ideals are now either put into the camps or disposed of!" John confirmed what he was saying,

"That's right! And they are so open about how numbers have to decrease for the world to survive!"

Lisa brought the meeting to a close by reiterating the importance of trusting Yahweh and that no matter what the enemy could throw at the world the people at the Ark would be safe and would see Yahshua again. She said,

"Thank Yahweh for you guys! Praise His name, that you held out!

Later on, that afternoon, Lisa and Charles were back in Ezra's room, deciphering the amazing discoveries that the Holy Spirit was revealing to them through the notes and writings of Ezra and Old Mr Carter and writing down all the experiences they had witnessed, when there was a knock on the door.

"Come in!" shouted Lisa and Charles together, causing them to smile. It was John again.

"Do you have a few minutes, Lisa, Charles? You should come and see this!" he said holding the office door open and beckoning them with his head to follow him. They stopped what they were doing and followed him down the corridor towards the front entrance and outside into the 'fresh' air. John pointed to the sky,

"Look!" he said, "They mean business now!" In the sky were line after line of 'trails' left by Jets. They were forming a grid of narrow white clouds over the entire sky. There must have been fifty to sixty lines forming this 'net' at ninety degrees to one another.

"What are they doing?" asked Charles, knowing that there could not have been a sudden large increase in overseas holidays!

John explained that for years 'they' had been systematically belching out toxic chemicals to form man-made clouds, claiming that it was in an effort to block the Sun's harmful rays and reverse the so-called global warming process. He said that many pilots had suspected that there was more to it than they were being told but had 'dutifully' carried out the orders they had been given.

"The ones who questioned, lost their jobs!" he said, "So most keep quiet for fear of the same or worse! But I never thought it would come to this! Look over here!" He took them to some nearby bushes.

"These leaves are starting to brown and curl up when they should be green and lush! Those trails that you see are toxic to life, they slowly poison the soil, the waters, plant and animal life."

"But what about food and water for people, surely that will be poisoned too?" asked Lisa.

"Of course!" replied John, "They have now created a modified gene in government grown crops that is resistant to the toxins and the same with an additive to put in their water but for the rest of us...." He held up the palms of his hands. "It's just part of their plan, I guess!" Lisa responded,

"God will take care of us here, of that I have no doubt, as well as all his people around the world that He is gathering right now. But why would they destroy their own essential supplies?" John replied,

"They have to control everything! People, Food, Drink, the weather; Life itself! Lisa and Charles shook their heads,

"Let's get back inside," said Charles thinking particularly about Lisa's condition, "this can't be good to breathe!"

They closed the door to the front entrance behind them, relieved to be safe underground in Yahweh's refuge.

John suggested people should limit how much they went outside now, unless it was very important and even then, people should wear a mask of some description.

"We have to inform everyone." Lisa suggested. "John, would you gather everyone together in the cavern and we'll talk to them,"

"This feels like we're living in some kind of apocalyptic movie!" said Charles.

"I know!" replied Lisa, "I've always known that the end would come but I never realised just how soon it would come or the kind of tactics that the enemy would use to destroy people.

They gathered everyone together and stood in the middle of the cavern. Charles began by informing the people that they were now going to have to spend more time underground because of the efforts of the N.W.O.

"But do not worry!" he exclaimed, "Yahshua told us that He is with us always and He will carry us through if we hold out until the end. He warned us of these things and we have to deal with it accordingly. We know that the enemy will try and destroy us, but Yahweh has given us this place and will keep us safe. You'll see! I know there are new discoveries just around the corner to bless us and make our stay here a journey to prepare us for the times ahead, when Yahshua comes back in glory to rule and reign with us! Keep faithful and loyal to the one who has the victory! Do not be concerned about those who can kill the body but cannot kill the soul but rather fear the one who can destroy both body and soul!"

Nods of agreement and 'Amens' could be seen and heard all over. Lisa felt the urge to capitalise on the moment.

"Oh, and one more thing!" Lisa said as she gripped Charles' hand tightly and took a deep breath.

"Charles and I are going to have a baby!" Cheers went up all around the cavern; it was just the 'tonic' everyone needed.

Lisa could see Tom and Jan Philips in the crowd just a few metres in front of them, along with all the others, applauding with all their might. How this group had grown to love one another like family was deeply moving.

Lisa and Charles eventually slipped away from the crowd and went back to Ezra's room and sat down for a well-earned rest. Lisa put her head in her hands and wept. Charles put his strong arm around her.

"What's wrong, sweetheart?" he asked, "Why so sad?"

She lifted her head and looked at him with her tear stained face. She wept,

"Can you imagine how those people are feeling? They followed us down here and now they find out that they have to stay in these underground caves, permanently! Or at least until Yahshua comes back! I never believed it would be like this, Charles! I thought that this was just the roof over our heads and not the place we would all be living in!" Charles got on his knees in front of Lisa's chair and held both her hands with his.

"I know how it looks, Lisa." he said compassionately, "but I believe what I said to everyone today! There is something just around the corner! God's timing is always perfect. He will come through and at least we are safe and alive!"

"I know you're right," she replied drying her tears with her fingers, "but sometimes it feels so hard and sometimes I worry about getting it right and that we are responsible for all these lovely people!" She looked at Charles' face filled with understanding and compassion.

"Oh, I don't know!" she continued, "Maybe it's just my hormones talking!"

"Yes, maybe it is! Come on!" he said standing up and helping Lisa to her feet. Let's go and have some fun with our boys!"

So, they spent the rest of the evening playing games and telling bad jokes with Luke and Josh. They talked about the great things of Yahweh and the fun times ahead that they would all have together, before settling down to a well-earned night of rest and peace. Luke and Josh went straight to sleep as soon as their heads touched the pillows. Charles and Lisa lay staring into each other's eyes. Through Charles' mind travelled the thoughts of all that had happened, the possibilities of what lay ahead and yet here he was married to and in love with the woman of his dreams.

"How are you feeling?" the protective husband asked the new mum to be.

"I'm good." she replied softly, "Just lying here contemplating and being so thankful that Yahweh gave you to me." They both smiled contently at each other and drifted off into a peaceful sleep.

Chapter Ten

Taken to the Edge

In the middle of the night, Lisa was woken from a deep sleep;

"Lisa.......Lisa," came a quiet voice,

"Yes Father?" she replied without opening her eyes, "I hear you!"

"Lisa, Lisa! It's me!" came the voice again, "I'm not the Father!" She immediately sat bolt upright.

"Then who are you!" She shouted and opened her eyes wide, ready to take on the demon from hell and waking Charles in the process.

"It's me, Eli!" came the now recognisable voice from in her bedroom.

"Eli!" she shouted, "I'm so sorry! What are you doing here?! You frightened me!" She got out of bed and hugged the angel who was standing in the corner of her room. Charles sat up in bed watching the proceedings.

"You have to come with me! Yahweh has something for you!" continued Eli. Charles questioned sleepily whilst yawning,

"Do you need me too?" Eli replied,

"Not this time, Charles!" Lisa hurriedly got dressed and followed Eli out into the corridor leaving Charles alone, sat up in bed. He shouted after them,

"Oh, that's great! You think you can come in here in the middle of the night and take my wife away with you, just like that?" There was no reply. "Yes, I guess you do!" he said to himself and lay back down in bed.

"It's great to see you again, Eli!" exclaimed Lisa hurrying down the main corridor, "Where are we going?"

"You'll see!" replied Eli, smiling knowingly. "It's great to see you too!" He looked different somehow to the way she remembered him; more Angelic somehow. His complexion was silk-like and he was clean shaven. His hair was still long but there were no jeans and overcoat this time, only a simple, bright white robe; how you'd expect an angel to look really.

As they opened the front door, Lisa started to explain to Eli all about the chemicals that the N.W.O. had been spraying recently but stopped mid-sentence as she realised that not only would Eli be totally aware of all that was going on, but also that she was talking to an Angel of Yahweh. Eli interrupted,

"The air is fine Lisa, don't worry, just follow." It was still light outside with the Sun and Moon having set but the glow from Orion still visible even though it was the middle of what should have been night.

Suddenly, the wind picked up and began to blow so strong that Lisa had to grab hold of Eli's hand. It was clear that something was stirring in the heavenlies. They walked up the hill to the meadow; leaves were flying all around them. Lisa noticed the figures of three men up ahead, again dressed in white, all with flowing black hair. Eli squeezed her hand to add a little security; to reassure her that everything was okay. The men stood staring at her and Eli, unmoved by the storm brewing all around them.

"What's going on?" Lisa asked, a little concerned at the way these men were glaring at her. Eli let go of her hand and in a flash, she found herself face to face with one of the men. She felt scared, as the man invaded her space and she turned to Eli for help, but he was nowhere to be seen.

"Come!" said the man and took her by the hand. As soon as they touched, she found herself in a room that was completely ablaze. The heat was so intense it took her breath away. She gasped, put her arms over her head then screamed,

"Charles! Eli! Help!" The inferno intensified; the heat multiplied; there was no way out; she couldn't breathe. She fell to her knees and covered her head. She gasped again for air and choked. All her thoughts asked in desperation,

"Is this the end? Am I dying?" She lay down on the floor, desperate for air like a fish out of water. With her last breath she whispered,

"Yahweh! help me!" She felt herself drifting away; blacking out. A voice said loudly and audibly,

"When you walk through the fire, you shall not be burned,

nor shall the flame scorch you, for I am Yahweh!"

In her semi-unconsciousness she recognised the scripture from Isaiah. The flames immediately backed off, the heat died down and an archway formed in the blazing wall of the room. She breathed; in and out; she was alive. She struggled to her feet and walked through the archway and instantly found herself back in the meadow. She looked herself up and down. Not a singe, not a burn, nothing! Bewildered and confused in her mind, she looked up to the sky and cried out,

"Why! Why! Don't you know I'm with child!"

Eli suddenly appeared by her side. She hugged him and cried tears of relief, sobbing,

"Why? Eli? Why?" The angel replied,

"Don't you know?" He looked at her with sympathy and said,

"All I can say, Lisa, is that nothing will stop the will of Yahweh! The word of Yahweh will not return to him void! Look!" He pointed across the meadow, where there stood another man. She looked at the man and within seconds they were face to face just as the first time.

"Come!" He said and took her hand. Instantly she was plunged into a raging icy torrent of rushing water. The pain of the cold water hit her immediately like a thousand knives.

The strong current rolled her over and over, filling her nose and making her choke. She tried to get to the surface, but the current kept pulling her down, dragging her deeper and deeper. Again, she feared for her life and that of her baby. She fought with all her might, but it was no use. She felt herself slipping into unconsciousness but somehow, with her airways full of water she bellowed out,

"Yahweh! Help me!" Immediately a voice said,

"Fear not for I have redeemed you: I have called you by your name; you are mine! When you pass through the waters, I will be with you; and through the rivers, they shall not overcome you. For I am Yahweh!" She shouted with all the power she could muster; water flowing through her nose and mouth,

"For you are Yahweh, my God. The Holy One of Israel, my Saviour!" The voice commanded,

"Stand up, Lisa!" She put her feet down and found a hard floor. Immediately, the waters calmed and the ground beneath her lifted up like a hydraulic platform. As she was coming up out of the water she looked up to the heavens and cried almost involuntary,

"You are who You are! You will be who You will be!"

In a flash she found herself in the meadow again. She fell to the floor completely exhausted but completely warm and dry.

Eli picked her up from the floor.

"Are you okay, Lisa?" He asked with a smirk on his face, "You look worn out!" She hugged her best angel friend again and said,

"You've no idea, Eli! And I can hardly swim!" He laughed which totally annoyed Lisa. She wanted to kick him in the shins but as she caught her breath back, she saw the funny side and joined him in the laughter.

"Listen," sniggered Eli, trying to cut short the fits of laughter, "I know I'm not allowed to help you at all here but answer me one question; Were you ever in danger? Either in the fire or in the water?"

"Too right I was!" exclaimed Lisa, "In both cases!" Eli replied with a serious tone of voice, the laughter couldn't have been further away,

"Really?! You still don't know why?!" He questioned.

"Well I think I do!" She stammered. "Both times God delivered me! Am I right?"

"Well let's see?" insisted Eli. He pointed across the meadow.

"Look!" He shouted. Lisa's eyes again naturally followed his gesture and she met the gaze of another man leaning against a tree. Instantly they were face to face, just like the previous two men.

"Oh no!" she cried, "Not more!" The man went to take her by the hand, but she pulled away sharply.

"I don't want to go anywhere with you!" Lisa protested but that familiar, calm, quiet voice spoke in her ear,

"Lisa, you have to understand, you have to know why." The fear dissipated immediately.

"Yes Father!" she replied, "Of course!" This time she held her hand out for the man to take. He took hold of it and said,

"Come!" They were both instantly teleported to Vantage point; the natural lookout point on the upper meadow. She loved the view from there. She looked across the water to what used to be Hightown. The land was so scarred. A great gash was carved through the countryside where the tsunami had hit, and the trees and plant life were dying as far as the eye could see. It was a sad sight considering how beautiful it used to be, but it still held a real feeling of awe and somehow, she knew it would return to its former glory.

"Lisa, come to the edge and look at this!" the man said in a gentle, coaxing manner. Trusting that he too was probably an angel, she walked with him. As she got close to the edge she could feel a tenseness inside of her. She was never very good with heights, but she wasn't going to show him that. Bravely she stood by his side; the drop was extreme, but she didn't look down. The man let go of her hand and pointed to something in the distance.

"Look!" he shouted. She looked to where he was pointing and not knowing what he was trying to show her, she questioned,

"What at?!" Then she suddenly felt a hand on her back give her an almighty shove and she toppled over the edge of the precipice. She screamed as she rapidly started to descend through the air towards the ground several hundred feet below; her arm and legs flailing as she went. The wind rushed into her face as she fell, causing her to lose her breath. She gasped for air as she struggled, plunging down towards the ground. Suddenly, an intense warmth filled her soul and the words of a Psalm came to mind and she immediately began to speak them out loud.

"Father, I trust You!" she said. "I lift up my eyes to the mountains, where does my help come from? My help comes from Yahweh, the Maker of heaven and earth. You will not let my foot slip because You who watch over me, You will not slumber; Yahweh You will keep me from all harm, You will watch over my life!"

As she spoke, a feeling of complete safety came over her and she knew that she would come to no harm. Still descending rapidly, she shouted,

"Amen!" Then she held out her arms like a bird and as she did the wind beneath her lifted her up just as when a parachute first opens. She was surprised as her descent ceased and she began to climb up through the air.

"I can fly!" she screamed as she glided over the tops of the trees. She could feel a hand holding her right hand but could see no-one. She smiled knowingly.

"I love you Yahweh! I love you!" she cried with joy, to which He replied to her spirit,

"And I love you too, Lisa"

Whatever was going on; whether this was a dream or her imagination or reality, she didn't care; she was determined that she was going to enjoy this. Round and round she flew, taking in all the scenery from a completely different prospective, staying up in the air for what seemed like an age. As she approached the Ark she could see Eli on the ground beckoning her to come to him. She thought to herself that she should pay him back a little, so she swooped over his head causing him to fall flat on his back. She laughed out loud as he shook his fist at her in jest.

"If this is what it's like in heaven," she thought to herself, "what are we waiting for!" She landed on her feet safely as though she'd been flying by herself for years. Eli dashed over to her,

"Well done, Lisa!" He said with a broad grin across his face, "I'm so proud of you! I was a bit worried earlier when you thought you were dying!" They both laughed. He continued,

"Now you understand what this lesson was all about?"

"Yes, I think I do! Well, at least I hope so!" replied Lisa, with a smile, combing her windswept hair with her hands. "Eli, when I was pushed over the edge, I felt like I was falling fast at first, but then it seemed as though I slowed down and began to fall in slow motion. Then I had a choice to make, either to focus on falling and be full of fear or put into practice what Father had already taught me. When I went through the fire and then the stormy water, I panicked at first and thought I was dying and then Father reminded me of scriptures both times. But when I was falling, I immediately thought of Psalm Twenty-One and I began to speak it out and I knew I was safe. That's when everything changed!" She smiled a victorious smile and continued,

"My thoughts then suddenly changed from thinking about the fact that I was falling to wanting to know what He was trying to teach me! So, I surrendered! Eli, what I'm trying to say is that we have to trust Him! We have to know His words and we have to do what they say! They have to be our compass, the direction we walk in!" She paused, thrilled with what she had learned from the Master. "When the world is in chaos or our own lives seem to be falling apart, we have to seek Him and do exactly what He tells us to do in His word! Those words are alive!

They bring life!

They can save our life, Eli!"

He laughed and said,

"I hear you, Lisa! And I couldn't have put it better myself! There is trust and there is *trust*! There is belief and there is really believing! If you believe, you obey! If you know what I mean."

He paused and looked at her lovingly. "Everything He does for you," he went on, "is for your good because He loves you. You've passed with 'flying' colours, Lisa! Well done!" Lisa smiled with happiness as he congratulated her. He continued,

"You know there are words that when translated into English just do not have the same impact as Hebrew and it is important to understand the difference. There is a word, 'Shema' which basically means 'Hear and Do!' This is the key for those looking to endure until the end; those who need to get through times of dire trouble. Take heed and listen carefully…. The book of Revelation chapter twelve says, that the dragon was infuriated over the woman and went off to fight the rest of her children, those who obey God's commands and bear witness to Yahshua!"

The angel looked deep into her eyes and said with great passion,

"Lisa, this is the safe place; the shelter of The Most High. Many, oh so many will fall away. Some will deny the eternal covenant of the Almighty; others will reject the Messiah, believing that their good works alone will save them! They will try to obey the covenant terms but deny the very life of it.... Yahshua!

Lisa, you must not be deceived! Meditate on those living words! Walk as Yahshua walked! Speak His words to your children, at sunrise and sunset! Keep His words within your heart and guard them with all of your strength!" She looked at him and nodded; filled with emotion and determination.

They walked back to the door of the Ark and Eli opened it for her. She went through and turned around to thank him for being a 'gentle-angel' but he had gone; disappeared; off on another mission no doubt.

She hurriedly walked down the corridor to her quarters, wanting to tell Charles all about her adventures but when she arrived at their room she looked at Charles, Luke and Josh; her family, all cuddled up safely in bed. They looked so peaceful. She decided to keep quiet and enjoy the opportunity to ponder in her heart all that she had learned. She thought to herself,

"Maybe this isn't for sharing? Maybe this was just for myself? Who would it believe anyway?" She felt an urge to go to Ezra's room and she had certainly learned to listen to the promptings of the Holy Spirit, so she quietly left the room and made her way along the corridor. When she reached Ezra's room she opened the door and walked inside, closing it gently behind her so as not to wake anyone. The fire was flickering as usual, giving out just the perfect amount of heat. She thanked her Father again for her test and all she had learned that night. As she looked over to her bible which sat open on her desk on top of all of her papers, she noticed it was open at the book of Isaiah. She examined closer. It was on chapter Forty-Three.

She read,

Fear not for I have redeemed you:

I have called you by your name; you are mine!

When you pass through the waters, I will be with you; and through the rivers, they shall not overcome you. When you walk through the fire, you shall not be burned, nor shall the flame scorch you.

For I am Yahweh, your God, The Holy One of Israel, your Saviour.'

"You are amazing, Father!" she cried out, her heart pounding with emotion; with the love that she knew He had for her.

She closed her bible and looked at the clock on the wall. It was still three o'clock! It was Yahweh time; that place where time doesn't exist. She shut the door behind her and went back to her quarters and climbed into bed with all her boys. She smiled to herself contently; truly blessed.

Chapter Eleven

Feed My Broken Lambs

The following morning, Lisa was sat in Ezra's room spending some quiet time with Yahweh, contemplating everything that had happened in the night. She made some notes in her book, trying to explain how she felt and what she learned as well as the actualities of what happened. As she gazed into the flames of the fire before her, she noticed that they seemed to be flickering in a strange way, almost in a pattern. Suddenly, a vision of a lamb coming towards her came from the fire.

"Hello," she said in a motherly voice, "who are you then?" The lamb continued to come towards her. As it got closer she noticed that it was limping and holding up one of its front legs. It became apparent that its leg was broken. The lamb came close to her and stopped. It was hungry and thirsty. She felt sorry for the lamb and put out her hand towards it. As she did, a voice in her head said,

"Will you look after this one, Lisa? Will you tend and nurture the ones who are broken?"

She replied, "Of course I will, Father! Of course!" Then the lamb disappeared back into the flames, leaving her wondering what Yahweh was saying to her. Surely, he didn't want her to look after sheep and wasn't she already taking care of the flock at the Ark? Her peace was suddenly interrupted and her thoughts on what she had just witnessed were completely distracted by a sharp rap on the door.

"Come in!" she shouted, gathering her thoughts. It was Jenny, who gestured for Lisa to come quickly.

"There seems to be some trouble outside!" She cried, "You had better hurry! Charles and John have gone ahead!" Lisa met Charles on the steps at the entrance crouching down with John. Charles whispered,

"John was outside when he heard voices and came in to get me! He thinks they may be armed!" Lisa noticed that John had a stick in his hand shaped like a rifle.

"They'll never fall for that!" laughed Lisa

"Shhh!" whispered John "Keep your heads down!"

The voices got louder and were nearly upon them when John jumped up and screamed,

"Stop, you lot! Stop right where you are!"

The whole group immediately threw their arms up in the air in surrender and shouting that they were unarmed and peaceful. John shouted at them in his natural police officer manner, demanding they all sit down and put their hands on their heads. Immediately they did as they were told.

"That's it!" he ordered, "Where I can see them!" He called over to Charles and Lisa who were still hiding from the potential confrontation.

"Charles! Lisa! Come on up!"

"They must be okay!" Charles whispered to Lisa, looking a little scared by all the army stuff.

"I'm sure they are!" agreed Lisa, "I'm sure they're nothing more than a bunch of God's people needing help, like us all. Come

123

on let's go and meet them!" Lisa ran up the steps and across the yard to John and the people with Charles following on behind.

"Wait for me!" he shouted, not wanting to appear frightened.

"Hello!" shouted Lisa as she got to them. They all turned and looked at her.

"Hello, Lady!" Said one of the men suggestively with a broad smile on his face. Charles stepped in to protect her.

"Who is your spokesman?" said Charles abruptly; he didn't like anyone being in the slightest way familiar with his wife. They all looked at each other. One of them spoke up, pointing to a guy at the front,

"He is!"

"Who me?!" questioned the involuntary leader, "Why me?!"

"You'll do!" said Charles and began his inquisition.

"Who are you all and where have you come from?"
John reminded Charles that they were unarmed and seemingly very friendly.

"That's great John, thank you." said Charles in his normal tone of voice.

"We don't actually know what we are doing here. We managed to escape the Police when we were all thrown out of church when we refused to sign the form." Charles interrupted,

"Thrown out of where?"

"Of Church, Man!" he continued, "Everyone has to go to church now! Whether you're a believer or not! Don't you know? Where have you been?!" They all laughed quietly. Lisa jumped in,

"Oh, you know! Building an Ark on a mountain! Surviving the tsunami that tore it down! Discovering an ancient world hidden underground, occupied by a three-thousand-year-old prophet! And apart from that we just grow vegetables!" The guy just stared at Lisa for a second and then the light seemed to come on and his eyes widened as he just 'twigged' something and the penny dropped.

"So, you're the ones! Holy smoke! We've found you!" He turned to the rest of the group and exclaimed, "It's them! The mountain people!" The group all 'high-fived' one another. Charles interrupted their celebrations and shouted above their voices,

"What do you mean?! You've been trying to find us?! What do you know about us?!"

The man replied, "You're famous, Man! In the words of Jessie James, you're totally wanted, man! Dead or alive!" He grinned as he looked at them in awe. "We, have all been thrown out of churches and escaped the police. I was in the woods one day after I managed to get away, when I came across this Jewish guy with a staff who told me to follow him and he'd take me to a safe place! I thought it strange, but the way he spoke, I had to follow him. The rest of us all met on route and we all followed him and he brought us here, and here we are!" They all laughed, cheered and high-fived again. Charles and Lisa looked at each other.

"Jewish guy?" Lisa asked, "So where is he now?"

The man continued,

"I've no idea! He was with us coming over the hill and he just seems to have disappeared! But I swear he was with us! He knew the way here!" Charles looked at Lisa. Who was this guide? Was he Eli or one of the other angels or was this Yahshua himself? Whoever it was they certainly wanted these people to find them.

"So, you were kicked out of church?" John asked. The guy answered,

"Yes Sir! We had to fill out a form before going into the main hall and I didn't like the look of it and neither did any of this lot! But when we complained they told us we had no choice but to fill it in. We turned to leave, and they came after us, so we legged it! The next thing we were being chased by the border police! They came running after us; shooting! I mean real bullets, Man! I don't know how we did it, but somehow, we got away! Will you help us, Man?!" he said looking at Charles for mercy, "We're so thirsty and totally starving!"

"Of course, we will!" said Lisa, "Follow us! We shouldn't be standing outside too long anyway. Don't you know it's bad for your health!"

"That's awesome!" declared the man and they all followed Charles and Lisa across the yard, "My name is Tony by the way," said the man, "Tony Franks, but you can call me Frankie Baby! Everyone does!"

"I'll call you Tony!" laughed Charles. Lisa responded,

"I'm Lisa by the way and this is my husband Charles."

"Yeah, I know!" said Tony smiling, "Like I said!" he made a funny gesture with his hands. Charles and Lisa just looked at each other. They all laughed.

They walked across the yard towards the steps to the Ark, when suddenly they were hit by the power of the Holy Spirit. One by one they fell to their knees under the anointing of the Most High God which was so powerful, it caused them to yield in submission to their maker and repent on the spot.

It was a wonderful sight; they were laughing, sobbing and crying out to their heavenly Father. Charles, Lisa and John just watched in amazement, praising Yahweh for the love that He was lavishing on these people.

Above their heads, something like a mist gathered and began to swirl around. It gathered pace for a minute or so before spiralling down and descending on the group of renegades. On their knees, they bowed to their Heavenly Father and begged Him for forgiveness for their sins. They gave their lives to Him there and then; no altar call, no prayer of Salvation, just a heartfelt cry of repentance to their God and a total acknowledgement of Yahshua.

"Well I guess they are well and truly on their way to being saved!" Charles remarked.

"They certainly are!" replied Lisa.

Slowly they got to their feet having been dealt with by their loving Father.

"Whoa! That was amazing!" cried Tony, "Now I know what the fuss is all about! God is cool!"

"He sure is!" agreed Charles, "Now let's get inside! We've been out here long enough!"

Lisa briefly pointed out where the house and buildings used to be and the unmissable swath that the tsunami left behind. They all just looked in amazement.

"There is so much to tell you guys!" Lisa said enthusiastically as they walked down the steps to the old door, "But let's get you all settled in first and get you something to eat and drink."

Thankful, they followed Charles and Lisa down the corridor but when they got to the main cavern they all just stood in awe at the size and height of the cavern and everything that surrounded them. All of their jaws just dropped open.

"Wow!" cried Tony, "Just Wow!"

Lisa introduced as many people as she could to Tony and his gang and arranged for food to be brought for them all, then stepped back and took Charles by the hand to go back to Ezra's room. She hadn't had chance to tell him about what had happened in the night or the vision in the fire yet, which seemed particularly relevant now. As they turned to go back up the corridor, Tony Franks came running after them.

"Charles, Lisa!" he said with a serious face, "I feel that I should probably be telling you about all the stuff that is going on out there!"

"Yes, you should tell us all, Tony!" Lisa replied, "But rest is what's needed first!" He replied,

"That sounds like a plan! Amen to that!"

Tony went off to his room, leaving Charles and Lisa to talk about the visions Yahweh had given her.

"That's amazing!" remarked Charles, "Father is so incredible!"

"That's right!" replied Lisa, "He certainly is!" They went back to their room to spend time with Josh and Luke and feed their babies before the day was over.

*

Later that night Charles and Lisa were sat in bed reading their bibles, with all the children tucked up in bed, when they heard a voice in the room;

"Charles...Lisa!" It was Eli the angel again lurking about in a dark corner.

"Oh no! Not again!" replied Lisa, still tired from the previous episode with her angelic friend, "What do you want now?!"

"I have to talk to you about something!" He answered.

"Okay," Lisa said slowly swinging her legs from her bed, "But let's make it less dramatic than last night!"

Eli smiled,

"You can both stay right there!" responded the angel, "I just need to give you a message from the Father."

"Awesome, go ahead!" said Charles.

Eli began;

"It's about those people who arrived tonight. They are the broken lambs that Yahweh showed you, Lisa, in the fire. Yahshua led them here and has entrusted them to your care, to nurture them alongside the others here in a way that you would with a delicate lamb or a baby of your own." They listened intently. He continued,

"You must shepherd them and lead them with gentleness as a true shepherd does, using a staff to guide them and using a rod on the wolves that would seek to devour them. You must teach with humbleness, gentleness and love; remembering that you have been given a great treasure with these people. These people are precious gifts with eternal value that the Father has put in your hands!" Charles and Lisa could feel the sincerity of his words sinking deep into their hearts. It was nothing they didn't already know but Eli had a way of reiterating the importance of the Fathers message.

"You are truly more powerful than you realise right now but not in your flesh, because you are purely a vessel to see the purpose of the Father fulfilled! All those who carry the heart of the Father, also carry the Spirit of the Father! By the anointing of the Holy One,

129

you are able to do all things; nothing will be impossible. Without Him you are empty and powerless!" The angel was now in full blown preaching mode;

"Your journey has taught you the depths of the words you read that day in your lounge in Hightown, that with God all things are possible! The key phrase in there is 'with God'. Now Yahweh knows that you long to tell the world that with God they too can do and be more than they ever thought possible. You long to share the treasures that you have uncovered! Yahweh has placed within you a passion to see others find those treasures; the truths that He has led you to. But understand this; only the Spirit of the living God can give understanding to the heart, only He can open ears and open eyes. So, you must not become impatient!

Remember the days, Lisa when you would take your sons, Luke and Josh, to the park and you would throw bread to the ducks and wild birds in the park. You would break the bread into small pieces and carefully scatter it for them. The birds would come and would eat until they were filled. Now imagine you had taken that big old loaf and come running into the park screaming, "Bread! Eat!" and then hurled the loaf at them. Those little creatures would have fled!" Charles and Lisa laughed at the picture Eli had so eloquently painted for them.

"The lambs are hungry, but you must feed them with love and gentleness. That, Charles and Lisa, is being a servant! You are serving Yahweh by serving them; delivering His words but then allowing His Spirit to bring understanding! There must be no desire to be right, there must be no impatience with those who take longer to understand than others!" Eli smiled, "Remember the words of Paul,

'Love is patient, love is kind. It does not envy, it does not boast, it is not proud. It does not dishonour others, it is not self-seeking, it is not easily angered, it keeps no record of wrongs. Love does not delight in evil but rejoices with the truth.

130

It always protects, always trusts, always hopes, always perseveres. Love never fails."

"Love cannot and will not fail! But if you bring the message of Yahweh with impatience, judgement, frustration, haughtiness or anger, you nullify the words that you bring because the foundation of Yahweh's eternal Torah is love. Without love all that you teach is void.... without love you bring the entire covenant to nothing! Paul in his wisdom also said,

"If I speak in the tongues of men and of angels, but have not love, I am a noisy gong or a clanging cymbal. And if I have prophetic powers, and understand all mysteries and all knowledge, and if I have all faith, so as to remove mountains, but have not love, I am nothing. If I give away all I have, and if I deliver up my body to be burned, but have not love, I gain nothing."

"So, Charles, Lisa. Go feed His broken lambs."

Before they could say a word in response, Eli had gone. He never seemed to hang around to get a reaction, he just delivered the message.

"Are we supposed to sleep now?" laughed Charles and they both sat there in amazement for a while before spending most of the night until the early hours excitedly discussing Eli's message.

Chapter Twelve

Beauty from Ashes

The following morning, Lisa woke with a deep stirring in her spirit and quickly got out of bed. She left the room and made her way to Ezra's room to spend time with the Father.

She picked up her bible to read and instantly felt His presence. The words of Psalm ninety-one immediately came to her mind and she opened her bible to read them;

'If you say, "The LORD is my refuge,"
and you make the Most High your dwelling,
no harm will overtake you, no disaster will come near your tent.
For he will command his angels concerning you
to guard you in all your ways;
they will lift you up in their hands,
so that you will not strike your foot against a stone.
You will tread on the lion and the cobra;
you will trample the great lion and the serpent.
"Because he loves me," says the LORD, "I will rescue him;
I will protect him, for he acknowledges my name.
He will call on me, and I will answer him;
I will be with him in trouble,
I will deliver him and honour him.'

As she read His words she heard His voice saying,

"Whatever happens, Lisa, remember I am with you always and everything is for the greater good. Even the turbulent times that you face, I will turn around. Many are the troubles of the righteous, but I will deliver you from them all!"

Lisa smiled, placed her pencil down and bowed her head in reverence.

"Yes Father!" she replied feeling humbled by His presence, "I hear you clearly! Thank you!" She kept her head bowed and thought about His words. She felt overwhelmed and excited that she was beginning to hear His voice so clearly, but slightly troubled at the content of the message. She had to remind herself that she had just read 'do not fear'.

"Good morning, sweetheart!" said Charles as he joined Lisa in Ezra's room with two cups of fresh, hot water! "It's not quite coffee but it's hot" He laughed.

"Oh, thank you, Charles!" said Lisa gratefully, "You're such a hero!"

Their Conversation was rudely and abruptly interrupted as Lisa was suddenly gripped by a sharp pain in her lower abdomen. She bent double in agony.

"Are you okay?" asked a frantic Charles, putting the cups down on the desk. He leaned over her, stroking her back as she bent over in her chair. As the pain subsided, Lisa lifted her head and smiled reassuringly at Charles.

"This happens occasionally in pregnancy, sweetheart!" she said trying to bring some calm, "It's not uncommon!"

Then she was hit with another 'bolt' of pain and then another. An overwhelming feeling of fear gripped her whole body causing her head to spin. What seemed like a thousand thoughts raced through her mind in an instant.

She argued with herself in her mind, knowing that the intensity of the pain she was feeling must signal that something was very wrong, but at the same time telling herself that there was no way Yahweh would allow bad to happen. She began to weep as the pain and the thoughts consumed her entire being. Lisa had friends who had suffered miscarriage, she always found their stories hard to listen to, even though she felt a deep compassion for them. She had no idea how those beautiful ladies had ever survived such a horrific thing. To her, they were superwomen and she marvelled at their strength. She could not imagine experiencing the anguish her amazing friends had gone through and surviving such an event, so she told herself that it could not possibly be happening to her.

"Charles, I need you to go and get one of the nurses!" cried Lisa.

"Come and lie on the couch!" insisted Charles and helped Lisa up onto her feet and started to walk her over to an old 'chaise' in the corner.

"You need to put your feet up!" he suggested calmly as Charles always did. Lisa fell to her knees as another surge of pain flooded through her. He held her, as she knelt on the floor in pain and he noticed a small spot of blood on the seat of the chair she had been sitting on.

"Come on, lie down!" he said lifting her off her knees,

"Let me take my time, Charles!" Lisa cried out.

"Okay, I'll go and find some help!" He ran out of the door and down the corridor shouting for a doctor or a nurse to come and help, he quickly returned with Sandra McAlpine, a general practitioner of old who had very quickly become the resident nurse at the Ark. As they entered the office, they found Lisa on the couch, writhing in pain and weeping profusely.

"What is happening, Sandra?" cried Lisa, "Why all this pain?!"

"I'm not sure, Lisa but just try and relax!" said Sandra in a calm, settling voice, "Let me take a look at you!"
She sat down beside Lisa on the chaise and examined her.

Suddenly Lisa made an involuntary push and a tiny baby was born; warm but lifeless.

It was over so quickly; no warning; no signs.

"Please! No!" Lisa cried, Please, don't let this be real! It can't be real!" She looked desperately at Sandra then Charles, "Tell me! Please! This cannot be real!" Charles wept profusely by Lisa's side as Sandra consoled them both and said,

"I'm so sorry Lisa." Lisa screamed,

"No! This cannot be!" She felt as though she was going to faint; completely overwhelmed, her mind wanted to shut out what was happening. Fear now seemed to mix with feelings of desperation.

"No!" she thought to herself, "This is one of those dreams and I want it over right now! Father, wake me up or do something! Make this stop, I need a miracle! Help me!"

Sandra hugged them both and wrapped baby up in a cloth and placed the little body in a box and gave it to Charles. She left the room to make Lisa a syrup drink to help with the terrible shock of what she'd just been through.

Charles and Lisa sat alone. They held each other and wept. Lisa looked at Charles.

"Why?" she whispered desperately. Charles couldn't answer. He wanted to comfort his wife and be the hero she always told him he was. Although he couldn't find the right words, he promised to stay by her side.

He held her tight in his arms and told her that somehow everything was going to be alright. He did not know what else to say.

"I know that God is with us, Charles." She said through her tears, "But why won't He answer!" Again, Charles could not reply.

Dark thoughts began to bombard her mind;

"How are you ever going to recover from this?"

"You are such a failure, Lisa!"

"Where is your great faith now, Lisa?"

"How can you ever help anyone?"

"This has exposed how weak you really are!"

"Time to wake up and get real!"

She cried out to Yahweh;

"Father, I don't know how to pray through this. I don't even know what to say. Please, please help me." As she called out to God, the visions she'd experienced of being consumed with fire and engulfed in the icy torrents came back to her. Everything she learned there was about trusting in Him with her whole heart and not just hearing his instruction but doing it as well. Now she found herself broken and allowing thoughts of complete defeat to overwhelm her. Again, she cried out,

"Father, I'm sorry! You told me not to be afraid and I am! But You also said that even through troubles You would come and deliver me!" Charles held her tightly. "So, I'm asking you, Father! Deliver me from this nightmare!"

*

Charles took Lisa to their bedroom; where she could get away from everyone and come to terms with what had just happened. She remained there for the next few days; hidden away. Charles tried to do his part; offering her food and water, which most of the time she refused and just lay silent on her bed with a constant flow of tears.

One morning, Charles sat alone praying in Ezra's room;

"Father, I need you!" He prayed, "Show me how to help my wife. I am hurting so badly at the moment, but I know that it is so much worse for her. Please help me to be who she needs right now!" A tear rolled down his cheek. "Father, I know that we haven't been through all that we've been through for it all to just end here! I know we have people to love and serve but right now neither of us have the strength. We need a miracle, Father."

He had just finished praying, when there was a light tap on the door. He got up and went to the door. It was Jenny. He opened the door and she went in.

"I need to speak to you both, Charles." she said, "I believe Yahweh has given me something to share with you both." Immediately his prayer came to mind and he wondered if this was the miracle he had asked for?"

"Yes of course, Jenny." he replied, "Lisa is in our room. Let's go and see if this is a good time for her. She's been so upset and hasn't moved for days."

"That's understandable," Jenny said as the closed the door to the office and walked towards their room, "and that's why I need to pass on the words He gave me this morning." Politely Charles knocked on the door to their bedroom. He slightly opened the door and said in a soft voice through the gap,

"Lisa, I know you're not feeling too good at the moment, but Jenny is with me and she has a word for us both." Lisa was sat in the corner of the room and really didn't want to see anyone. Her first thought was to say, "thank you but no thanks", but something inside her caused her to say,

"Okay, come on in." They stepped inside, and Lisa came out from her dark corner. Although Jenny didn't say anything, Lisa's appearance took her by surprise. She was a shadow of the Lisa she knew; her hair was unkempt, and her complexion seemed pale and drawn.

"Pull up a bed and sit down." said Lisa trying to put on a smile and a brave face. They perched on the edges of two beds as they had no seating in their room. Jenny started, holding back tears of sympathy for her dear friends.

"Charles, Lisa, I don't have the words to tell you how grieved I am. You probably feel very alone right now but I want you to know that there isn't a person outside of this room who has not been weeping with you. None of us understand why this has happened but one thing we have all learned through this journey together is that Yahweh never fails us. I can't imagine how anything good could possibly come from such a tragedy, but I do know that Yahweh is able to bring beauty from ashes." She paused for a moment and held both of their hands. She continued,

"I have a simple message for you both that you will know well, but this is for you,

"He brings comfort to all who mourn,
and provides for those who grieve in Zion;
to bestow on them a crown of beauty instead of ashes,
the oil of joy, instead of mourning
and a garment of praise, instead of a spirit of despair.

That they may be called trees of righteousness,
The planting of Yahweh, that He may be glorified."

She looked at them both and said,

"He has told me that your healing will come quickly when you bury your baby." Jenny hung her head in sadness; somewhat relieved that she had said what she needed to say but uneasy with causing them anymore pain. It had certainly not been easy to deliver the message.

Up until then, the thought of a burial hadn't crossed Lisa's mind, but she realised that it was inevitable. Lisa replied, seeing Jenny's uneasiness about passing the message on,

"Thank you for bringing that to us, Jenny, I just need a little time to process."

"Of course," said Jenny, standing up, "I will leave you two in peace but just remember, we all love you both, very much!" She slipped out of the room. The tears that she had held back while in the room with Charles and Lisa, now came flooding out of her as she walked away from their room. She cried,

"Oh Father, help them! Please give them strength and as you have said, may their healing come quickly, in Yahshua's Name."

Back in the bedroom, Lisa and Charles pondered on the words that Jenny had brought to them both and they agreed that it was time and decided to bury baby immediately.

They took the little box and went to look for a suitable place outside. Instinctively they walked to the place where they got married on the meadow. It had wonderful views and was a special place for them both.

"This is the place" said Lisa, softly. Hot tears streamed down Charles' face as he dug a small hole. He couldn't believe he was having to do this, after the joy he had just a short time before.

As Lisa knelt down to place the box inside of the ground, everything inside of her wanted to run away with that little box and keep her baby safe. It felt so wrong to leave her baby there in that field, all alone.

She sobbed and held the box close to her chest,

"What am I going to do now, Charles? I can't do this!"

He put his big arms around her and then helped her to place the box in the ground.

As the box touched the earth, rain started to fall, as though Yahweh himself was weeping with them. They filled the hole with earth and planted a small tree to mark the spot.

They knelt together by the grave, crying out to their Father for comfort, when suddenly the Sun's rays broke through the clouds and shone through the rain with intensity, as it would on a perfect hot summer's day.

Two rainbows appeared, one in front of them and one behind them. Colours seemed to project out from the rainbows and filled the whole sky. They gazed in amazement at the wonder before them and they felt a beautiful, comforting warmth enfold them both. It was as though someone had just placed a warm blanket over them. The warmth touched them both deeply, healing their open wounds. Lisa began to cry out,

"Father, I don't know why! I don't understand! But I know, I know that you are faithful!" Warm tears mingled with rain as she lifted her face to the sky and cried out,

"Abba, Father!" she sobbed, "I trust you! I know our baby is yours! And although I don't understand, I still thank You and I love You. I will always praise You, my Yahweh. I don't know how this pain can ever be healed but I'm asking you to help me! Please tell baby how much we love her! I know she will be safe in your arms now." Charles hung his head and wept bitterly.

Then, they both heard the words from within their hearts, "She is your Treasure in Heaven, waiting here for you."

The words brought an incredible comfort. Lisa sobbed again. This time with a hopeful heart she cried out,

"I thank you Father, you give, and you take away! I thank you for the few months that I was honoured to carry this little treasure! I thank you for the joy she brought us both. I love you!" Charles, still sobbing, echoed his love,

"Amen, I love you too!"

The healing had begun. Lisa was astonished at the strength that rose up from deep inside of her, when just minutes before she felt as though her heart had broken into a million pieces.

"Only Yahweh can do this!" she thought to herself. From somewhere deep inside she felt a knowledge that there would be healing. Right now, it was the smallest glimmer of hope but was enough for her. It was like a lifeboat that would rescue her through this storm.

They wandered back into the Ark, where all their friends, family and fellow believers were waiting for them. It felt so homely for a giant hole in the ground. There was a reason why all this had happened, and Lisa knew it. Although, as yet she didn't know why, she knew she had to trust Him. Yahweh was their guide, their deliverer, their defender and their friend. He was the reason they were being redeemed and saved from the hell that people of the world were witnessing.

Although Charles and Lisa had taken an emotional battering, the days ahead seemed to be filled with hope. They began to resume their study, receiving revelation from His word and getting new light on old things.

One evening, Jenny knocked on Lisa's door and opened it before anyone could reply.

"Lisa, you have to come quickly! No time for questions!" she exclaimed and hurried back down the corridor, with Lisa in pursuit.

"What's wrong?" asked Lisa, shouting as she ran.

"Just follow me!" cried Jenny, "It's amazing!"

"What is?" questioned Lisa in return, as the rounded the corner into the main cavern to meet a huge crowd who had gathered around the 'practise' area where the doctors and nurses resided. People stepped aside as Jenny came running through followed by Lisa. The sight that met Lisa was beyond comprehension; a sight that truly measured the mercy and faithfulness of Yahweh. There in the practise with nurse Sandra, was Charles and in his arms were two beautiful, perfect babies. She stood still about ten feet away, with her hands over her wide-open mouth.

"What?... I mean, who's are these?" Lisa asked, not daring to believe why Charles was standing there grinning holding two new born baby boys.

"Well," replied Charles, "They're no-ones!" Lisa looked confused but said nothing. Charles continued, "I found them in a small cave at the far end of the deep tunnels. No-one here knows anything about them! All I can imagine is that someone has left them here to be protected from all the trouble outside! But I have no idea!" Lisa replied with a thoughtful look on her face,

"I, I mean normally, I'd say we should call the police but obviously we can't do that!" She looked all around at the faces smiling at her.

"No, we can't!" said Sandra, "So will you take care of...."

"Yes!" interrupted Lisa before Sandra could finish her sentence, "A thousand times, Yes!" Everyone cheered as her face glowed with joy and she ran over to them and cuddled them both in her arms. She had so longed to hold her baby and now she had two to pamper.

"Thank you, Yahweh!" she cried, tears of joy rolled down her cheek, "Thank you!"

Charles wrapped his arms around them all. Luke and Josh, who had been so saddened about their little sister, now jumped for joy with their parents. It seemed their family was now complete. The crowds eventually dispersed, and Lisa took her babies back to their quarters with Charles and the boys.

Miraculously, Lisa found that she was able to nurse them herself too, which was such a blessing for her. She was truly the proud mother again.

"What shall we call them, Charles?" asked Lisa sitting up in bed, a baby in each arm.

"I have absolutely no idea!" he replied, "But I'm sure Yahweh has that in hand!"

She looked at the babies in her arms and noticed that one of them was making a fist with his right hand and poking through his fingers she saw a tiny corner of what looked like a piece of paper. She gently unfolded his little fingers. He was grasping a small section of a page out of a bible.

"Where have you had this from?" she asked. She opened out the crumpled paper and saw a verse from the book of Ezekiel.

It read:

*15 The word of the LORD came to me: 16 "Son of man, take a stick and write on it, 'For **Judah**, and the people of Israel associated with him'; then take another stick and write on it, 'For Joseph (the stick of **Ephraim**) and all the house of Israel associated with him.' 17 And join them one to another into one stick, that they may become one in your hand.*

"Ephraim and Judah?!" she cried, "Is that their names?! Ephraim and Judah?!" As the words left her lips, the babies reached out and grabbed each other's hands.

"Look Lisa!" Charles remarked, "Look what they're doing!"
Lisa smiled,

"That's all the confirmation I need!" she said, "Ephraim! Judah! Welcome to the Ark!"

Chapter Thirteen

Old Men will Dream

Halfway through the night, as Lisa was feeding one of her beautiful babies, she looked deep into his eyes.

"You are so beautiful!" she whispered,

"Which one are you?" she asked softly,

"Are you Judah?" The baby smiled.

"Or are you Ephraim?" The smile left his face, so Lisa asked again,

"Are you Judah?" The baby smiled again. "You are, aren't you!" She marked him with a 'J' on his forehead with her finger and he smiled again. Charles rolled over in bed and half woke when he saw Lisa sitting up.

"Look, Charles!" Lisa announced quietly. Charles sat up. "Meet Judah!" Baby smiled again. "He does that every time I mention his name. "Judah, this is Daddy!" More smiles.

"What amazing names!" remarked Charles tickling Judah under his chin. Lisa laughed,

"Yes, God chose them! You said that He would have it in hand and He did! In the baby's hand!" Charles laughed and replied,

"Yes! That's right! How cool! I love it!"

Lisa stroked Judah's face,

"Oh Judah!" she sighed, "You are so handsome!" The baby smiled once more. His eyes sparkled with delight.

"Wow how cute!" said Charles now fully awake, "I wonder if Ephraim does the same!" Lisa replied,

"Let's find out." She put Judah down and went to get Ephraim who had the same beautiful eyes, but he didn't smile at all when his name was mentioned. In fact, he looked quite grumpy. Charles said it was because he was made to wait for his milk. They laughed together; something that they hadn't seemed to have done in quite a while.

After feeding Ephraim, Lisa put the twins down and they all went back to sleep.

Hours later, she woke suddenly from a vivid dream; just how Yahweh had spoken to her in the past. Charles woke at the same time, sitting immediately upright.

"Wow! That was some dream I've just had!" he said, "Lisa, I need to tell you about this! Yahweh has spoken to me in a dream!"

"Yes, me too!" replied Lisa, smiling, "Do you want to go first?"

"No, after you!" said Charles being the gentleman. Lisa replied,

"I know! Let's have some food and then we can go to the office and have a time of prayer and then we can talk about our dreams, it'll be easier there."

"That sounds like a plan!" said Charles and they busily got themselves and the children dressed. Luke and Josh were eager as usual to run off and find some play mates. Judah and Ephraim were cuddled up together in a warm blanket and so without disturbing them, Lisa carried them to Ezra's room. Charles got some food for them both and for Sophie and the boys, then made his way to Ezra's room.

It was always so lovely in their study, so warm and cosy with the fire burning away. The babies remained snuggled up as Charles and Lisa began to tell of their dreams.

"I'll start then!" said Lisa looking directly at Charles, their chairs facing one another. "In my dream I was…." She was stopped in her tracks by a knock on the door. Charles opened it, to find Sam on the other side who said apologetically,

"I'm sorry to interrupt you guys but I just had to come and tell you all about this dream that I had last night!"

"Yes, me too!" came the voice of Jim from behind Sam.

"And me!" shouted Connie over Jim's shoulder.

It seemed everyone had been dreaming overnight and they were queuing up to tell.

"Well you'd better all come in then!" laughed Lisa making some space for everyone. Charles moved the chairs to one side, when there was another tap on the door. This time it was Jenny and Ben.

"Sorry to bother everyone," Jenny said, "but we have both had amazing dreams last night that we thought we'd better come and share with you!" Everybody laughed.

"What's so funny?" asked Jenny

"Amazingly, that's why we're all here, Jenny!" Lisa laughed, "So come on in!"

They all shuffled around in the small, cosy room and found a place to sit. One by one they shared the dreams that Yahweh had given them in the night and Jenny wrote them all down as she was the only one who could do 'shorthand'.

Lisa began by explaining that in her dream she was watching the Moon, the Sun and the stars all spinning around together in perfect harmony and then at certain points they would all stop, perfectly still and then a horn, a Shofar was blown. When the blast subsided they all continued on their paths until they froze again followed by another Shofar being blown and so on, seven times in total. The whole dream was repeated three times.

Jenny was next to share and, in her dream, there were seven clocks all ticking together. One by one the chimes went off until finally they were all ringing together. She said that it felt incomplete until they were all chiming; they rang for a common purpose.

Connie followed and related how she saw a family in an attic pulling out a beautiful wooden chest that, from the outside looked wonderful and ornate. They were very sentimental about the chest as it had been in the family for many generations and at the same time every year they would pull it out of the attic. Inside the chest was nothing but broken and meaningless items but somehow even these items seemed dear to them.

This family also had another chest that was also kept in the attic. It was very old, dusty and dull and at first glance, didn't look nearly as impressive as the other chest, but inside there was gold, silver, precious gems and treasure of all types. The family never discovered the treasures in the second box because they simply never opened it. They were so familiar with the first box and had come to love it so much because it had been used by the family for generations. So, they left the second chest untouched, unopened and unloved.

There was also a box in Jim's dream. He had been cleaning a room out when he came across a new box which had a new lock on it but there was no key to it. He searched around the room but could only find an old rusty key that must have been very old indeed. Amazingly, the old key fitted the new lock and unlocked the new box. When he opened the box, it was full of the most wonderful treasure.

Charles spoke next, and, in his dream, he had been invited to various gatherings and each time he attended these gatherings, he miraculously missed some catastrophic disaster going on outside of the building that held the gathering. When he arrived at each event he was pre-warned that the disaster was about to take place and so remained safe until the trouble had passed.

Sam dreamt that a small but strong, evil man was tearing up calendars in complete rage and anger. While he was doing this, evil creatures of all shapes and sizes were throwing huge black blankets across the sky to hide the Moon, Sun and stars.

This only left Ben, who had sat very quietly throughout the whole meeting. He held his bowed head in his hands before looking up at everyone. He gazed at all the faces that were staring at him waiting for him to tell his dream. He attempted to say something, then stopped quickly and put his head back in his hands.

"Come on, sweetheart! Tell yours!" said Jenny sympathetically, "Don't be embarrassed!"

"I'm not embarrassed!" responded Ben, "It's just that...." He stopped again.

"Go on, Ben!" insisted Lisa, "Tell us what's on your heart! We are all one here!"

"Well...." said Ben hesitantly, "When each of you told us about the dreams you had last night, all I could hear was an interpretation in Hebrew. I know what your dreams mean, and I feel Yahweh wants me to tell you the interpretation before I tell you about my dream,"

"That sounds good to me!" said Lisa looking around the room for approval. Everyone nodded.

"Totally!" agreed Charles, "Ben, go ahead!"

"Well it's like this....... Lisa, your dream. The Sun, Moon and stars represent the signs that Yahweh put in the sky for us all to see to mark the appointed times or 'Moedim' as they are called in Hebrew. The Shofar heralds the beginning of each biblical feast of which there are seven in total. This being repeated signifies they are 'set' times. It's very interesting Lisa, that in the book of Genesis in chapter one verse fourteen we read that,

'God said, "Let there be lights in the firmament of the heavens to divide the day from the night and let them be for signs and seasons and for days and years;"'

"Now I'm sure we are all familiar with this?" Everyone nodded.

"However," he continued, "we have another situation of 'lost in translation' because the word 'season' isn't entirely accurate; it should read 'appointed time' or 'set time' or 'festival'. It is interesting that the festivals allow us to predict Yahweh's plans. Some having already been fulfilled, others yet to come." He looked at Jenny and said,

"Your dream, is very similar. The clocks are set at the appointed times for the Holy days and biblical feasts. The alarm goes off to announce each one. They all go off together as a special announcement that something is about to happen. They are prophetic too; each one is a picture of Messiah Yahshua in His first and second coming and collectively they pronounce the fulfilment of the Will of the Most High!" He turned to Connie,

"Yours, Connie, is interesting and is very much connected to everyone else's dreams!" Ben continued. "The whole world has been distracted by counterfeit festivals, counterfeit Holy days! They even call them 'holidays' but they have no meaning, they are fake! They glitter and shine in the way the first and loved chest, gets people's attention even though, the truth is right in front of you. Truth or Tradition! A choice people need to make. Again, referring to biblical festivals versus man made traditions." The room was silent, engrossed in Ben's words. A truth was being revealed to them all.

"Sam!" he said smiling, "That small evil looking man was indeed the evil or lawless one, the accuser. He and his demons do everything they can to hide the signs that Yahweh put in the sky for us. He has torn up the biblical calendar and replaced it with one that hides the appointed times which is why the demons were frantically trying to cover up the Sun, Moon and stars. A simple dream but very powerful."

"Just like me!" joked Sam, "Simple yet powerful!" He got an "Amen" and a pat on the back from Jim. Everyone laughed. Ben turned to Charles.

"Yahweh says to us through your dream, Charles, that when we observe or attend his appointed times or feasts, we come under His protection. He has told us all many times to observe His Sabbaths and Feasts. Many of His promises hinge on them. The knowledge of His Festivals give us insight into His plan of time and pre-warn us of things to come. They help us to be aware of the time we are in so that we are prepared."

He turned to Jim.

"And finally, Jim, the key to unlock the new is the old. The old key unlocks the new box. The Old Testament or unlocks the New Testament and one can only function with the other! You need both! Then you will find treasure and the answers to what can look like a riddle and can be very difficult to understand. Peter warns us in Second Peter, three verses fifteen and sixteen of this, saying that the Apostle Pauls letters can be very hard to understand if we lack understanding from the Old Testament." He paused and looked at them all. You could have heard a pin drop. Ben continued,

"Yahweh is requiring of His people to return to the ancient paths, the ancient times in terms of His Instructions, His Sabbaths and His Feasts. They were never taken away, just hidden. He wants us to put His word on our hearts to enable us; to empower us by His grace and the power of the Holy Spirit. It's the old and the new coming together. You cannot understand one without the other. They become complete when they are used together." Again, he paused. Yahweh was talking to him.

"Stand at the crossroads and look! Ask for the ancient paths, ask where the good way is and walk in it. There you will find rest for your souls!"

Lisa was fixed on the words of Ben; this was the key she believed that was missing for God's people. Suddenly, everything that Ezra explained to her, about Abraham and the ancient paths, made sense.

Jenny then demanded,

"So, tell us about your dream, Ben!"

"Yes!" insisted several people.

"Let's hear it!" said Sam.

152

"Okay, okay!" said Ben, cowering down at the barrage of words being fired at him. He cleared his throat. They all waited in anticipation. He continued,

"In my dream, we were all at a banquet, sat around a large table. Some of the platters on the table contained wonderful delicious foods but other platters contained things that were not food. They contained some unusual items like pebbles, screws and other odd objects. The strange thing was that most of us attempted to eat these strange items along with the real food. We seemingly had no idea that these other objects weren't food. I knew immediately what my dream meant, but it seemed odd that I should have it at this time considering the only food we have here is a plant! The meaning of the dream was this:

We need to be able to distinguish between the holy and the unholy, the clean and unclean, including foods. Just as prophesied in Ezekiel forty-seven verse twenty-three, which is a prophecy concerning the End Times and the Millennial Kingdom. The reason I felt that this is a strange time to reveal these things is because these are principles that mankind should have always applied, but now we are in the last of the last days, we don't know how many more of Yahweh's feasts we will be able to celebrate, if any! With regard to food, we have no way of eating unclean foods even if we wanted to! I don't know how much time we have, but I do know that we have little left on this earth and we cannot afford to beat about the bush with any of the things that Yahweh has been revealing to us all today. We need to pray and study together more, and soon!"

Jim interrupted,

"Before you go on, you're not telling me that I was sinning by eating bacon are you, Ben? Because all that stuff was dealt with at the cross! Look at Acts chapter ten! How do you explain that? I respect your Jewish roots, brother Ben, but I'm a gentile. I was never under

those rules to start with and now more than ever, I'm free of them!"
Ben replied,

"Wow Jim! I've never heard you be quite so outspoken! You sure are passionate about your bacon!" he laughed. Jim mumbled,

"I certainly miss it!" Everyone laughed, and Ben continued,

"Jim, Acts chapter ten, or Peter's vision, is not about food! Read on, Peter goes on to share the interpretation for his vision, it was all about the gentiles! The enemy has deceived the children of Yahweh right from the garden, telling them that Gods instructions don't apply. Isn't it funny that he used food then too! A pig is not food! Neither is a shrimp, or any scavenger, for that matter! He tells us clearly what is and isn't food. Yes, all foods are clean, but some things just aren't for food! They have a different purpose!" He paused, hoping that he had finally got his point across. He continued, "To be true followers of Messiah, we must learn how He lived and follow Him. We are to walk as He walked!"

Jim interrupted again,

"Ben, believe it or not, I like a simple life and a simple faith. This past year, I feel like I've lived from one challenge to the next! I move to a house in the mountains against the advice of every friend that I have! I survive an earthquake! I've seen the sky torn! The sun and moon standing side by side! The house ripped down and washed away to reveal caves where a weeping prophet seems to have lived for a thousand years! I've eaten chicken flavoured plants that grow out of walls in a cave and now to top it all, now I'm being told that during my 40 years as a Christian I've missed a whole bunch of things that matter and that I am supposed to learn them now, even though it's possibly too late! But....," he said with a sigh, "I do know that, as you've said, we are in the last of the last days and I don't have the time to be stubborn about this!"

"Amen!" said Connie. Jim just gave her a look and continued, "So, if you're willing to take some time to give me a crash course in this stuff and walk me through the scriptures, so I can see for myself whether or not what you are saying is true, then I'm willing to consider what you're saying!" Lisa agreed,

"Yes, we all need to study together and bring out the truth from the scriptures. We can learn so much from each other. Ezra explained some of this to me some time ago and I sort of understood then, or at least my spirit did!" she smiled, "But now it's so much clearer! This is the way forward and I believe that our time is limited, or we could miss the boat!" They all agreed and arranged to meet together daily in the cavern.

They all got up and left the office while Lisa took her two babies and began to feed them. She picked up Ephraim first to make him happier and see if he would smile in the way Judah did.

"Hey Ephraim!" she said, but still no smile. He was definitely more serious than Judah. She wondered if it maybe had been the same way with their namesakes. As she was feeding Ephraim she heard a voice say,

"Ben was right, Lisa! I need you to observe and remember my Commandments, including Feasts and Sabbaths. They will direct your path and shine a light in the darkness. Your obedience in observing My Holy days will be like signposts that will help you through the darkness!" She replied,

"Thank you, Father, We will!" Lisa looked down at Ephraim,

"Wow!" she said, "You are a big boy, aren't you?" Still no smile but for the first time she noticed his hair; a beautiful dark brown. "What a handsome boy you are, Ephraim!" When she was feeding Judah, who always gave her a beautiful broad smile, she noticed that he too was growing very well and that his hair was exactly the same colour as Ephraim.

Charles came back in.

"Have you thought about Ben's interpretations yet, Lisa?" he asked.

"Oh yes!" replied Lisa, "And they are totally spot-on!"

"I agree!" said Charles, "It feels so good to be getting back to His truths."

"Yes, it does!" agreed Lisa, "By the way, have you noticed how big these boys are getting?"

"Not really," replied Charles, "why?"

"Oh nothing, don't worry!" said Lisa, "But they seem to be putting a lot of weight on or maybe I'm just feeling weak."

Charles sat down at the desk to continue with his studies while Lisa was enjoying time mothering her wonderful gifts.

She was amazed how 'good' her babies were. Even though Ephraim was a little grumpy, they never seemed to cry much apart from a little whine when they got hungry. She looked at them and thanked Yahweh again. What treasures they were, real gifts from Him. She looked at Ephraim's thick eyelashes;

"Wow! You're going to be a good looker!" she said to him. She looked at his brother,

"And you!" she said to Judah. She shouted over at her hubby, who was writing notes studiously,

"Charles, have you noticed what good looking boys we have?"

"Uh?!" replied Charles engrossed in his work. She conceded,

"Oh, never mind! It's just Mum and baby stuff anyway!"

She looked down at them again. They were indeed beautiful. She laid them down on the blanket and took some warm water to give them a body wash.

It was while she was bathing them that she noticed something truly incredible; they had no navels! She looked closely, one then the other just to make sure. Sure enough, there was not a navel between them.

"Wow! How can that be?!" she said to herself, checking again to make sure she wasn't losing her mind. "What is it with these babies?!" She remembered how Charles had said he had found them and that someone must have left them there for their safety, but she was beginning to realise that it wasn't a human that had left these babies; they had come from the Almighty; her babies hadn't been born of normal birth, they had been created.

Chapter Fourteen

News from the World

A week had passed since Yahweh had given her the twins and every day, Lisa made some sort of comment to Charles about how much they'd grown, but Charles somehow hadn't noticed.

Their hair was becoming really quite thick and even though Lisa knew that was not uncommon for babies to have a lot of hair, she had never seen it grow so fast on a new born. She was convinced too that in the night she had felt a tooth coming through each of their gums.

It was the Sixth day and their first Sabbath, to be observed at the Ark, was coming up. Everybody was preparing for the following day of rest. Sophie had agreed to baby sit with Lisa's new babies while Lisa knuckled down with the ladies in the food preparation area who needed to prepare twice as much as usual. It was amazing how busy everyone was just surviving without the aids of the modern world. So, the Sabbath was certainly welcomed by all.

 Lisa was storing up some of the meals that were to be put away for the following day when Sophie came running into the food preparation area.

"Lisa! Come quickly!" she yelled, "It's the twins!"

"What's wrong!" Lisa screamed frantically at Sophie running down the corridor towards her quarters.

"You have to see this, Lisa!" replied Sophie, "It's amazing!" She ran into their bedroom and what a sight met her eyes. Judah and Ephraim were both standing up playing with Jenny.

"What?!" cried Lisa, the twins both looking around at her as though they had done something wrong. "How?!" Lisa was almost speechless.

"Just how old are your twins, Lisa?" asked Jenny laughing.

"I've had them just a week today!" Lisa replied not knowing whether to laugh or cry. In the end she decided to laugh and said,

"I knew they were growing fast but this is crazy!"

Charles came running into their bedroom and stopped in his tracks; mouth wide open.

"Now do you believe me!" cried Lisa.

"How can...? How is this...?" Charles spluttered.

"As I've said many times, Mr Michaels," reasoned Lisa, "With God all things are possible!" They all laughed out loud; Judah giggled with them; Ephraim remained straight faced.

Jenny went back to work, and Sophie took Luke and Josh off to play, leaving Lisa and Charles sat alone on the floor of their bedroom, watching their week-old babies playing, sitting down, standing up and even attempting to toddle.

"Why are they growing so fast, Charles?" Lisa asked curiously.

"I have no idea!" replied a bewildered Charles, "Only Yahweh knows why! But there must be a reason!"

Eventually, Lisa went back to her task in the food preparation area, taking orders from Connie who ran that 'ship' with high efficiency.

Everything was just about complete, when a sound echoed throughout the Ark. It was sundown, time for 'Shabbat' and Jim was blowing his trumpet that he had painstakingly made from various scraps of wood and metal that he had found lying around outside. It had a quite daunting ring to it but it was certainly unmistakeable. All over the Ark, people put down their tools or brushes or whatever they had in their hands. They took off aprons, overalls and smocks; the day of rest was upon them.

Over the next twenty-four hours they would honour their heavenly Father with the 'Shabbat'. There was a huge atmosphere of excitement and anticipation; for what no-one knew or cared; it felt so good to show their love and obedience to Him. An area of relaxation had been made in the main cavern that was spectacular. Giant beanbags of a type had been made from spare mattresses, for people to recline on, in an area where people could share stories and testimonies of the great things God had been doing in their lives. People relaxed in their own quarters as well and spent quality time with their families and loved ones. Everyone helped themselves to food and took whatever they needed. It was beautiful to see and be a part of.

Through it all, Yahweh was lifted high; some worshipped Him with songs and verse. There was a new intimacy in prayer and worship that countless people claimed they had felt.

At the same time, the equivalent to sundown on the Seventh day, the Shofar blew again, and it was over. The First day had begun; in a way, it was sad and over all too quickly, but they all knew they had next week to look forward to.

The following morning the people continued with their daily lives and the running of the Ark.

Charles and Lisa took time each day to encourage Tony Franks and his gang. Tony, had been to church on and off during his life but had never truly grasped what it is to have a relationship with Yahweh. Most of the group had a basic knowledge of the gospel whether through religious studies during their school years or the odd visit to a church on a special occasion, but like Tony, they hadn't been taught that Yahweh desires a relationship with each one of us, or how they could live a life that pleases Him. Charles and Lisa talked to them about their purpose and encouraged them to discover truths in the scriptures and how to grow in their faith. They seemed to soak it all up like sponges. Some gave testimony, how God had spoken to them through the Sabbath. It was so good to hear.

Suddenly, they all heard a sound that they hadn't heard for a very long time; a sound that cried out danger to them all; that everybody knew meant trouble. It caused the whole crowd to 'shut up' in immediate silence. It was the ringing of a mobile phone. It echoed through the heights of the huge underground cavern, the crags and crevices reverberating the worldly sound.

"Oh, excuse me, everyone!" said Tony Franks answering his phone, "Hello! I can't hear you, it's breaking up! I don't have much sig...."

"Switch that off!" screamed John as he snatched the phone from his hand and threw it on the ground. Tony picked it up out of the dust.

"Hey, that's an expensive phone!" he protested.

"I don't care how much it cost! You've just given our location away! That thing will have a GPS on it that tells everyone, that connects with it, where you are! Who called you?!"

"I'm not sure," said Tony looking at the handset, "it looks like one of those government numbers, I guess they're looking to see where I am."

"And you just told them!" replied John angrily. He snatched the phone from Tony again, ripped the back off and tore the battery out of it. "They've been looking for us for ages! Helicopters go over most days!" John sighed, "Remember what you told us when you came here? That we were famous! Wanted dead or alive! Well, now they know where we are!"

Tony hung his head, totally remorseful.

"I'm sorry man!" he sobbed, "It hasn't worked since the earthquake! They must be fixing things out there!" John put his arm on Tony's shoulder.

"It's my fault, Tony," John responded compassionately, "I should have checked when you arrived!" Tony looked distraught; aware of the seriousness of the situation.

"It was a genuine mistake, Tony." Charles reiterated, "Let's focus on what we need to do now because the chances are high that we will be getting a visit soon!" They all sat down. Tony admitted,

"There may be more going on than you realise!" Lisa asked,

"So, tell us what you know, Tony! Tell us what we may have missed?"

"Well," replied Tony, "What do you know?" He didn't wait for a reply, he just continued, "I mean, did you know they're now demanding that people take the chip, rather than just recommending it."

"The chip?" John responded, "You mean an implant device that can track a person twenty-four seven, like they've put in animals for years?"

"Well its different now, man!" Tony went on, "The chip for the people is not an implant as such, it's more like a plaster.... erm a patch, you know like when you're trying to give up the smokes, with the big difference being that this one won't come off! It kind of welds to your skin! The chip for government people is different, that's more like the old animal implant; it contains more info, and some say, even a poison for anyone going AWOL!"

Charles and Lisa looked at each other; they had seen this patch in the vision they had at the camp.

"They've been going on about it, day and night, ever since the disasters! The chip this! The chip that! The chip the other!"

"Chips with everything then!" laughed Sam. No-one laughed this time. The atmosphere was too serious. Sam mumbled about quality humour not being appreciated. Jenny gave him a friendly jab in the ribs.

"That's right!" Tony went on. "They recommended it at first, after so many people lost their homes and belongings when the earthquakes struck, but now they are demanding that everyone takes it. They're saying that no-one will be able to buy or sell anything without one. They won't be able to do anything or go anywhere! Everyone who pledges allegiance lives to the new world order gets one for free. That's the gimmick at the moment but soon it will be 'chip or camp!' Next it will be 'chip or die!' It's inevitable!" John responded,

"It already is, Tony!"   Charles and Lisa nodded in agreement. Tony carried on,

They want to control everything!" He looked at his feet, holding back tears.

"It's all happened so fast that it's hard to believe, I know!" he said, shaking off whatever triggered the emotion, "My life used to be so simple; I worked for local government in Monhampton; working five days with the weekend off. But since 'Abrahim' came on the scene so much has changed."

"Who's that then?" asked Charles curiously.

"Yacov Abrahim! You know?!" replied Tony deliberately.

"Who?" said Lisa laughing.

"Yacov Abrahim! You've never heard of him!? My word, you are out of it up here!" laughed Tony in return. "He was initially brought in as an EU rep after the disasters and now he even seems to advise the Prime Minister! They say he's taking over the whole world!"

"What one person?!" Jenny remarked sarcastically.

"Oh yeah man!" said Tony emphatically, "Oh yeah!"

He paused, "This dude gets what he wants! Every-time!" He paused again and looked around the room. Everyone was intently listening to his words. "And since the prophecy, things started to get real nasty!"

"Prophecy?!" questioned Lisa, "What prophecy?!"

Tony carried on,

"Someone...." he exclaimed, raising his voice up a notch or two in obvious anger towards this person, ".... gave a prophecy to Abrahim, that a birth was going to take place that will bring an end to the New World Order and now he wants to destroy this child when he finds him!" Lisa and Charles looked at each other. Tony continued, "So they have made it law that there must be no more births until further notice! If women are found to be pregnant they are forced to have an abortion. They claim it's because of financial crisis and massive over population. All children who are already born and are under one are now property of the government and are taken away from their families to be raised in a so called local 'care' centre!"

"That's terrible!" Lisa responded, "How can they get away with that!"

"Well they so are, man!" replied Tony, "They say it's for their protection and provision because each family who takes the chip is given enough 'dosh' to provide for the adults and the children who are one year or above. I guess this will go on until they think they've found the one they're looking for!"

"But how will they know this particular baby?" asked Charles, "What will they look for?"

"Well," whispered Tony looking around, "I don't think they've figured that out yet! They think it'll be obvious when they find him but all they know right now is that this baby is going to be born soon or at most is one year old!"

"But there are thousands like that, in this country alone!" exclaimed Lisa concerned for her twins.

"They don't care, man!" Tony replied. "It's all part of their plan!"

Chapter Fifteen

Found

Everyone thanked Tony and they all left the room. Lisa and Charles went back to Ezra's room.

"Oh, my goodness!" whispered Lisa to Charles. "They are so evil! And now they know where we are! But there is no way Yahweh would have allowed Tony to come if this was going to harm His people and His twins!"

"That's right!" replied Charles. "And He definitely did! I know He wanted him here!" Lisa nodded and said,

"Yes, He gave me that vision of the lamb in the fire and he could not have been brought here just to give us away! But maybe we should figure out a way of hiding them just as Moses' mother had to do, even Joseph and Mary had to flee with Yahshua! Let's pray because Yahweh is in control, we just have to do what He tells us to do!"

Lisa sat in her chair next to the fire and Charles pulled his chair close to her.

"Yahweh will protect them you know." said Charles in a soft gentle voice, "He always has, right through history."

"I know," replied Lisa, "and He has spent so long teaching me how to trust. So, I must."

"That's right," responded Charles. They held hands, bowed their heads and began to pray but as soon as Charles said the word 'Father', they both heard His audible voice say,

"Charles, Lisa!" They both instinctively opened their eyes and stared at each other.

"Yes Father?" Lisa replied. He continued,

"Don't focus on the mark of the lawless one. I want you to focus on My mark!"

They waited; but nothing more. Lisa repeated,

"Your mark?" Then she said, "Thank you, my Father, thank you!"

"What does that mean?" asked Charles.

"It's His ways!" replied Lisa, "His Sabbath, His Word, His Commands! Look!" She opened her bible, to the book of Ezekiel Chapter twenty and read:

"I am Yahweh, your God; follow my decrees and be careful to keep my laws. Keep my Sabbaths Holy that they may be a sign between us. Then you will know that I am Yahweh your God!"

"That's amazing!" exclaimed Charles, "Why haven't I ever noticed this before?"

"I know! But at least we are making a start!" replied Lisa, "Come on we'd better get back, it's getting late,"

They closed the door and went back to their room. Lisa went to pray with Josh and Luke while Charles got ready for bed. She then tucked the twins up for the night before jumping into bed and cuddling up to Charles. Even though much needed to be discussed, Charles was soon snoring away.

167

"Oh well!" Lisa thought to herself as she closed her eyes.

In the early hours of morning, she found herself drifting in and out of sleep. In her mind she could hear a child talking. She suddenly sat up in bed. Was it a dream or was it Josh or Luke? She heard it again,

"When the end meets the beginning

and only two choices are left,"

she looked over to where the voice was coming from.

"Only when we jump do we realise our wings

and there we learn to fly!"

She looked over to where the voice was coming from and to her amazement, she saw Ephraim, lying on his back staring at the ceiling, talking away, seemingly prophesying. Lisa kept quiet. She tried to wake Charles gently as not to disturb the prophecy, but it was no use, he was 'dead' to the world. Ephraim continued,

"Why are we so afraid? Afraid of disappointment?

Afraid of fear itself? Afraid to fail, afraid to even try!

Why don't we let go? Why don't we follow?

The calling from deep inside,

drowned out by the voices outside!

The choices we have,

the wide and the narrow path:

One paved with gold and filled with every imaginable treasure: The

Other an uphill climb which begins with a cross to carry."

168

Lisa sat there, her mouth wide open, staring at Ephraim. Was she dreaming, or did she just hear a two-week-old baby prophesying? This time, Lisa thumped Charles in the arm to wake him. Charles groaned and spluttered. She whispered,

"Wake up! Look at this!" Groggily Charles sat up.

"What's happening?" he asked, wearily rubbing his arm.

"Look!" said Lisa again, pointing at Ephraim.

Ephraim rolled over to look at them both and smiled.

"It's a miracle!" insisted Charles, "He smiled!"

"No! Not that! He's been prophesying!" Lisa whispered loudly. Charles looked at her with a 'you have really lost it this time' look.

"What?!" He said in bewilderment. They both listened but nothing could be heard. Charles put his head back on the pillow and said,

"Are you sure you weren't dreaming?"

"Of course I'm sure!" answered Lisa a little annoyed at Charles' unbelief. Then she thought to herself,

"Am I sure? It is a little hard to believe!" She lay down next to Charles who was already asleep and snoring again. As she lay there pondering on the whole incident, she heard another voice saying,

"It's so easy to take the easy!"

She sat up immediately. It was Judah this time! He continued,

"The narrow looks so lonely. Surely simplicity is reward?"

She thumped Charles again who woke easier this time. She shook him and pulled him upright to witness the miracle. Judah continued to Charles' amazement,

"You hear the call but you're so afraid to fall,

keeping a grip on control and you won't let go,

you won't let go!

But can't you see? Don't you know?

It's only when to you are taken to the edge,

only when you are pushed;

only when you fall will you realise you have wings.

It's there you learn to fly!"

Lisa and Charles just stared at Judah, totally gob-smacked. These two babies were totally astonishing, almost straight out of the bible. They were indeed messengers of the Most High.

"Told you I wasn't imagining it!" gloated Lisa. Charles replied sarcastically,

"Yes, I'm sorry I didn't believe you that our week-old babies were prophesying!" They both laughed and put their heads back on their pillows.

"Why are they here?" whispered Lisa, "I mean, did they just come to get me through the heartache with baby or is there much more to all this?"

"I have no idea!" whispered Charles in reply, "But they are certainly cute!" Lisa thumped Charles playfully again and they tried to get back to sleep. They both tossed and turned not able to stop the sight of the wonder that they had just witnessed from churning around in their minds.

"I can't sleep!" moaned Charles.

"Me neither!" Lisa replied, completely awake.

"Let's get up!" suggested Charles and without replying Lisa climbed out of bed and got dressed. They took the twins with them to the office to continue their studies. Judah and Ephraim walked alongside them, holding Mum and Dad's hands as they went, waddling in their nappies.

Lisa and Charles sat down in the office and settled down to study Ezra's notes, part of which were titled, 'The mark of Yahweh', while the twins played on the rug in front of the fire.

"There is so much that I haven't seen before!" Charles remarked. Lisa agreed,

"I know exactly what you mean, Charles!" she replied, "Things I have read before that somehow I just never understood, now makes so much sense!"

Taking a break, Charles sat looking at their twins playing together. He remarked,

"I wonder what Yahweh has planned for these two?" echoing their thoughts from earlier. Ephraim turned to Charles and said from his delightful little mouth,

"We are to speak the word of Yahweh, the Most High Elohim, the holy one of Israel. We will be witnesses to Him and help prepare the way for His return. Before he sent Eli and the angels, now we are here to lead you to the place, the place where the end will begin." Charles and Lisa's eyes welled up as Ephraim spoke. At the same time, the door opened, and Sam came in. He was just about to say something but stopped dead in his tracks when he saw Ephraim talking away and immediately backed out of the room and closed the door. Ephraim continued,

"The time is near and surrendering to Him is going to save your life." He stopped talking and carried on playing with Judah, who said nothing but just smiled. Lisa dried her eyes and ran after Sam.

"Did you want me, Sam?" Lisa shouted after him, seeing him hurrying down the corridor. He stopped, turned around and walked back to Lisa, as pale as a sheet.

"Did I just see what I think I saw?" asked Sam shaking nervously, "Were you having a conversation with a two-week-old baby?"

"Well, so what if I was?" smiled Lisa.

"Oh nothing, I guess," replied Sam, "I thought I'd kind of seen everything at my age but then I guess I haven't seen anything yet!"

"That's about right, Sam." said Lisa and gave him a hug. "Now what was it you wanted?"

"Oh yes!" said Sam, "I almost forgot! Everybody's waiting for you in the meeting room!"

"This early?!" Lisa replied, "It must be important! I'll get Charles and sort the twins out. You go tell them we're on our way!"

There was quite a 'buzz' in the room when Charles and Lisa arrived. Tony was relating more stories about the society that was being built outside, intriguing everyone at the thought of what they had left behind.

"So why are we here so early this morning?" Charles asked.
"Tony has more to tell us!" said John, "We had a heart to

heart last night and found out that there is more that he needs to say." Tony carried on,

"Yeah, that's true!" He cleared his throat and began,

"Yesterday, when I said that I worked for the local government, I don't think I quite painted the right picture." He paused and looked at Charles, then continued, "I couldn't say at first cos I didn't think you'd take me in cos when I escaped from Monhampton, I had been with the police for nearly ten years, after spending six years inside, in prison for doing drugs! I have been working as an informer!" You could hear a pin drop. Tony looked around at the faces before him; the people that had taken him in and cared for him, where many others hadn't. "Have I let them down?" he thought to himself, "Have I betrayed them?" He carried on with his message,

"When the disasters happened, many seaside towns and cities around the world were destroyed and that was the point where everything changed. It was amazing how quickly that change came about! It was as though they were sort of waiting for the disasters to happen! Out of nowhere there seemed to be hundreds of 'crisis centres'; supermarkets and warehouses that had been closed for years; empty churches, all converted within days, even hours to these fully functioning crisis centres. The military were suddenly everywhere. A whole new society being created out there." A few mumbled in agreement. Tony continued, "The governments of the world had a big meeting and decided, in their infinite wisdom, that 'religion' was the main reason for wars around the world, that in the name of 'peace' there should now be just one! And man! Has that caused chaos? No-one can worship freely now! Worship can only take place at the state churches and anyone objecting to this, are being put in camps all around the globe and people are being forced to accept this new religion. Even though I was very reluctant to continue my job I had to. I was forced to continue; no choice. As an informer in the

173

police force you are now told to obey orders or you die and so does your family, so that's what you do; you obey! I did up until I saw my family go through the camp system and ultimately give their lives to this so-called god of light." Tony broke down crying, "I mean I don't know much but that's Lucifer, right?" He looked around the room for confirmation, which he got. He continued,

"At first, they sounded so convincing, cos what they say is so similar to what we heard in church about the old law being done away with. They say that the old law is full of outdated rules that a loving god would never burden people with. And get a load of this...." He gestured dramatically, ".... They say that Jesus started the new law and that they are just enforcing it to bring an end to hate crimes and wars. Now, I hadn't been to church a lot. I've believed for ages and I thought that would get me my ticket to heaven, you know? But one thing I did know, was that this message was way off. If you don't buy into their message at that point they put you through their six-week counselling program!" Tears streamed down his face,

"I couldn't do it!" he cried, "I just couldn't say 'yes' to what I knew they wanted me to say 'yes' to! All I could think about was what if they're wrong! I mean, why did Jesus say stuff about sending people who practice lawlessness to hell? I was too scared of making a mistake that big!... I mean if I'm going to get it wrong I'd be better off being wrong about keeping Gods commands, right? So, if I signed up to this declaration about chucking away the 'old law' as they called it, I could end up on the wrong side of God! And that is not cool!" He dried his eyes with his sleeve,

"Anyway, when I saw my wife and kids say 'yes' to their demands, my whole purpose ended. They were gone, and I no longer had a reason! They were my reason for living!" He paused, his head bowed down. He took a deep breath and carried on,

174

"They destroyed my family, so that I had no life, no point, no purpose. I believe God must have heard my cries because when I managed to escape, I was planning on ending it all! I was walking through some woods, when this Jewish guy with a shepherd's crook thing, told me to follow him and that he knew somewhere safe. It was all a bit weird, you know but something about him made me want to follow! As I walked with him we found more people along the way, they'd all legged it too!" He smiled, "Funny bunch! A bit strange like me! They all had amazing stories of escape and painful stories of loss or being betrayed by wives, brothers, parents and even kids. We were a bunch of broken and bruised outcasts led to this amazing place where we feel like we've been put in a big family!"

He lifted his head and looked at everyone; "Please forgive me for my phone, it was stupid of me. I'm so sorry!" Lisa couldn't stand it any longer and got up, went over to Tony and hugged him, followed by Charles and everyone else.

"God has heard yours cries, Tony!" said Lisa crying along with him, "And that is why you're here! He will reward you for your bravery and obedience. He's seen your heart. You will help many people, Tony. You are far more powerful than you have been led to believe! I mean some of the things you just said about how you knew their message wasn't right, you could have taught most of us a thing or two!" Everyone agreed and went to sit back down.

Tony continued. "But now we have a problem, cos they probably know where we are and are probably on their way here, as we speak! If they see any babies they will take them! So, we've got to protect your twins at all cost!"

As they were talking, they were interrupted by a thumping on the door. It was a red faced, out of breath Justin.

175

"They're here!" he gasped, "Police! Lots of them! Helicopters, guns and everything!"

"Speak of the devil!" cried Tony, "I am so sorry!"

"Okay, everybody!" John shouted above the ensuing chaos, naturally taking up his role, "First thing is to keep calm!"

"Charles! Tony! Come with me! Justin, go with Lisa and Jenny! Get those babies safe! Everyone else do what you can to calm those who don't know what is going on! And remember.... Yahweh is in control!" John led the way out of the room, followed by Tony and Charles.

They ran up the corridor toward the front entrance.

"We have to try and talk to them!" demanded John running towards the main door. "Maybe they will be in a good mood!" The three of them reached the door to the Ark. They could hear the Police shouting orders to one another outside.

"Let's pray before we open the door and step outside!" Charles said, while breathing heavily.

"Father, I know you are in complete control but help us now! Help your people!" A voice answered,

"Keep calm, Charles! Let them in! Trust me!"

"He's told me to let them in and trust Him!" Charles said as calmly as he could under the circumstances.

"Then that is what we do!" replied John, "Trust!"

Charles opened the door and they walked up the old steps to the yard, to be greeted by armed police pointing guns in their direction.

"They're guards from Monhampton!" whispered Tony, "I recognise them!"

An officer shouted through a loud hailer,

"Stand still all of you! Put your hands in the air!"

They did as they were told. Then the officer shouted,

"Franks! Is that you?!" Tony replied,

"Yes! It's me! Put them guns down, man, and let's talk!"

The sound of safety catches going on could be heard all around and Charles and John breathed a sigh of relief.

"We've been looking for you, Franks! We tracked your phone and assumed we were going to find you injured or being held hostage. Why have you been gone so long and what are you doing here?" asked the officer in charge walking over to them. As he stood by them, Tony replied,

"I don't know! I got a bit lost after the storm and then the next thing I found myself in the fields outside here! Weird really! And then these people helped me out!" The Policeman looked cagily at Tony and said,

"So, you're not being held here?"

"No, these people saved my life!" replied Tony. The policeman continued,

"Well you'll need to come back with us! They need you and your wife is looking for you!"

"Yes, sir!" replied Tony, "Of course, sir!" The officer in charge looked menacingly at Charles and said,

"While we're here, we're looking for someone who we believe may be hiding amongst one of these sort of groups, so we will need to search this place! Let us in now and we'll cause no more fuss than is necessary!"

"Of course!" said Charles, "Follow me!"

Chapter Sixteen

A New Salvation

Charles and John went first down the steps, back through the door and started off down the corridor but were soon barged out of the way and pushed to one side by the rushing policemen following them.

"Don't mind us!" shouted Charles, as a train of policemen sped past them.

"Come on!" John urged them, "Keep up with them or they'll wreck the joint!"

"Over my dead body!" shouted Charles running after John, who shouted back,

"Yeah it might just be if we're not careful!"

They could hear the cries and screams from the people as the police entered the main cavern.

Lisa, Sophie and Jenny had taken the boys and the twins to the deepest part of the caves to hide themselves and sit it all out while the men dealt with the Police. Charles went to lock the door to Ezra's room to make sure nothing was messed with in there but when he arrived he noticed the door was slightly ajar. He stuck his head inside, to see a young policeman searching through their things, pushing books and papers left and right without thought.

"I beg your pardon, young man!" he shouted, "This is a private room!" He replied arrogantly, with a smug grin on his face,

"I don't care whose room this is! I've been told to search everything, so I will!"

"Well, show some respect!" Charles responded angrily, "These are important things to us!"

"I'll do what I want!" replied the young officer pushing a whole row of books off the shelf. Charles took the offensive and grabbed hold of the officer's arm and pulled him away from the shelves that he was ransacking. The officer pushed Charles violently to one side throwing him against the wall. Charles fell to the floor and the officer continued his destruction of the room. Charles got back on his feet to retaliate when a calm voice in his head said,

"Pray, Charles!" He stood behind the young man and closed his eyes and prayed to his God. As soon as he did, he began to involuntarily shout out at the young officer in heavenly tongues and the door slammed shut by itself, scaring both Charles and the policeman. Suddenly, the 'fire that never went out' roared like a lion; in a way he had never seen before. The fire had always remained constant, just a beautiful gentle flickering flame, but now it was like a menacing inferno. The flames leapt from the fire and completely consumed the young officer; totally enveloping him. He screamed with fear as the fire turned in a small tornado as it engulfed him, bringing him to his knees. Hundreds of tiny tongues of fire ran over his body and settled on him. Charles, concerned for the young man's life stepped towards him, about to try and put out the fire when he noticed his face; instead of him having a grimace of pain as you would expect for someone who was on fire, his expression was one of absolute joy and peace. The fire of God was delivering him and cleansing his soul dealing with him in a way that only Yahweh could.

He was loving him into submission. As the man knelt there covered in flames, his hands raised in worship, Charles noticed as small object fall from one of his hands to the floor. It was a small micro-chip. He recognised it from how Tony had described it being the 'chip' given to military personnel. Not only had Yahweh stopped this man from destroying Ezra's room but He had also redeemed this man from the fires of hell, even in the midst of all the chaos taking place. Charles picked it up and placed it in the drawer of the desk before dashing out to find Lisa and the boys and help protect the twins, leaving the policeman there enjoying his encounter. He ran through the corridor toward the main cavern in the direction of all the shouting and screaming, worried that he was already too late.

Although he knew the Police would surely find the twins, deep inside he knew they would be safe, that Yahweh's will would be done. Still, he ran as hard as he could. As he got to the tunnels in the furthest part of the caves he started to shout his wife's name. He rounded what he knew to be the final bend of the corridor, when his shout was finally heard.

"Charles! In here!" He ran towards the cave at the end of the corridor, to be greeted by Lisa with her finger over her mouth. She stood there with Jenny, Sophie and the boys at the entrance of the dimly lit cave and beyond her, was a circle of policemen all looking at the twins. His heart sank; He was too late! They had found them!

"It's incredible, Charles!" whispered Lisa excitedly, "They are looking for babies, but look at our twins! They have grown again! Look!" Charles said nothing; he just stared at the twins astonished at the sight before him, they looked at least five years old!

The twins were in the middle of the circle of police turning around slowly, mesmerizing the policemen with words that had to come from heaven itself. The police were totally transfixed; frozen solid.

The twins suddenly stopped when they saw Charles and ran to him.

"Daddy!" they shouted in unison and hugged his legs. As soon as they stopped their 'chant', the policemen returned to a normal state.

"These kids are way too old, we're looking for a child under one!" he shouted, "Let's get out of here!" They put their guns away, turned around and left the cave; the sergeant ordering them to continue their search.

Everyone stood amazed. Everything was in Yahweh's control, absolutely everything. She realised there and then that she had just witnessed two major miracles: one, that the twins had supernaturally grown way past the age of this baby they were looking for and two, if she had been pregnant right now, she and her unborn baby would both have been in great danger.

Lisa took the twins and calmly walked back to the main cavern where the police were re-gathering.

"This place is clean!" said a police officer to his sergeant, "No-one has found anything! No babies! No pregnant women!"

The sergeant turned to Charles and said,

"We'll be back to interview you all here, regarding your identification procedures and your re-location. You do know that you are not supposed to be living out here?! We are rebuilding local towns since the disasters and you will all be given new homes! You don't have to live like this! But for now, our priority is to find a person who is wanted for crimes against the state and so we will leave you here for now and someone will be in touch with you soon!" He thanked Lisa and Charles for co-operating and ordered his men to leave. They filed out down the corridor, past Ezra's room and out of the main door. Charles closed the door behind them.

There was a huge cheer from the people as they heard the door close. They had escaped what looked like certain captivity and certain death. Tony came running out too; he had been hiding in his room, hoping that they would forget about him being there.

"How does He do it?!" exclaimed Lisa. Charles replied triumphantly,

"Well, He is the creator of the Universe! Praise His Name!"

Suddenly, Charles remembered something and gasped as he put his hand to his mouth.

"The policeman in Ezra's room!" He ran towards the corridor leading to the room with Lisa, hot on his tail. John and Tony followed too, wanting to ensure there was no further trouble.

When they got there, they opened the door and stood amazed at the sight before them. The young policeman was sat cross-legged in the middle of the room on the floor reading a bible. The fire had resumed to its normal state of flickering in the fireplace.

When he saw Charles and Lisa, he put the bible down and said with a grin on his face,

"Hi! How are you all?! I hope you don't mind but I just had to borrow this book!"

"We don't mind at all!" replied Lisa walking into the room and sitting on her chair next to him, "So what happened to you?" Charles interrupted,

"We were just fighting in here when the fire leapt out and saved this young man!" Lisa stared at her husband.

"You were fighting?!" she asked, not knowing this side of the man she was married to.

"Well, yes!" Charles replied, "He was messing up your shelves! So, I had to stop him!" Everyone laughed. The young officer proceeded to explain to everyone, everything he had witnessed in great detail and they all listened intently to his story of being filled with the Spirit of Yahweh in such a dramatic fashion. He was a changed man.

"Would it be alright if I stayed here with you all?" He asked politely, "As I cannot carry on the life I had out there! I would be the first in line for elimination!"

"Of course, you can!" replied Lisa and Charles together. Lisa continued, "What is your name?"

"I'm Pete." He replied. Lisa introduced herself and everyone else in the room. "We'll ask someone to find you a room and get you some food." She said to the grateful Pete. John interrupted the niceties,

"Just a slight situation, Lisa!" he stated, "He will have one of those dreaded 'chips' in his arm! They will be able to track him and come back looking for him!" Charles opened the drawer of the desk and took out the chip he had put in there earlier. He said,

"This fell out of his arm when he was consumed with the fire of God!" He showed it to John and Tony.

"That's it!" said Tony, "That's the police edition!"

"I had to have that thing!" explained Pete, "I didn't choose it, I didn't even know I was getting it! They told me I was having a vaccination that would stop me getting sick because of the water pollution!"

"We need to destroy it!" exclaimed John.

Without hesitating Charles threw it into the fire and a small puff of green smoke emitted from it.

"That's the best place for it!" He laughed, "Give it to Yahweh!"

"One more thing!" John said to Pete, "Could you take off all your gear and we'll dispose of that too!"

"Gladly!" said Pete and took off his belt of weapons and accessories and gave them to John followed by his communication devices.

"Wow!" said John, looking at the plethora of instruments of order, "They equip you well these days!"

Lisa took Pete down to the main cavern and introduced him to Connie who gave him the obligatory hug.

"Can you look after Pete for me Connie, he's new and will need some food and a room too."

"Of course, I will!" said Connie, "It's my pleasure!"

Lisa went back to the others in Ezra's room where they were going over the day's events, laughing and praising Yahweh for His goodness.

"He sure is amazing!" commented Tony, "When I used to go to church I never saw anything like this!"

"None of us did, Tony" replied Charles, "There are many times since we have been at the Ark that I have looked back and wondered what it was all about back then!" Tony and John wandered off to get something to eat while Charles and Lisa stayed in the room.

"Do you fancy a walk?" asked Lisa.

"You know, I would love one!" replied Charles, "Shall we sneak outside for a while?" Lisa nodded and said,

"That would be wonderful."

Charles stuck his head through the door and crept up the steps to make sure the police had all left, while Lisa stayed at the entrance. He signalled to her to follow.

"The coast is clear!" he shouted jubilantly. They walked around the grounds remembering and reminiscing. They'd had a lovely, even if brief time there before the disasters with many special memories. They held each other by the hand as they wandered up onto the meadow where they were married. They recalled the wonderful day when they made their vows to each other and stood gazing across the panoramic view, which, even though it had changed a lot, was still dramatic, if not as beautiful as they remembered.

"It's been an interesting marriage we've had so far, Mr Michaels!" remarked Lisa.

"It sure has, Mrs Michaels!" replied Charles, "Never a dull moment, that's for sure!"

They wandered passed their baby's grave and noticed the little tree that they had planted there had grown substantially and was completely covered in blossom. Other plants and trees around them were withering, from the effect of the chemicals that were being sprayed into the skies, but their tree was flourishing. Lisa smiled, remembering the word that Jenny gave to her when she went through such brokenness after losing baby. She quoted,

"A planting of Yahweh that He may be glorified!" They both stood and admired the tree, still holding hands.

"He loves us all so much!" Lisa said as she smiled, gazing up into her husband's eyes, "And none of this would have been the same without you, dear Charles.... I love you!"

"I love you too, Lisa" replied Charles. He stroked her hair and caressed her cheek. "You are the most beautiful thing on this planet, Lisa Michaels and I thank God that he brought you into my life!"

They kissed each other passionately, only to be interrupted by a rumbling in the distance which sounded like far off thunder.

"What was that?!" asked Lisa. Charles replied,

"I've no idea! But I think we should get inside! It sounds like there is a storm coming!"

Chapter Seventeen

Out from the Darkness

Charles was just closing the door behind them, when he heard another rumble in the distance only this time it was a lot louder. He went back up the steps onto the slab of the old house, to take a closer look. He could see a glow in the distance over the mountains and a plume of smoke rising from it. It looked like an explosion of some kind had taken place. Then he looked up into the sky to see a sight that made him stand in awe. It was like a heavenly firework display; some sort of meteor storm.

Charles stood staring at the sky mesmerized by its beauty,

"It must be Orion's belt finally reaching earth." he said to himself, "At least we'll be safe down here!"

No sooner had he said 'safe', when a huge fireball flew right over Charles' head, screaming and crackling as it went, seemingly coming from nowhere, causing him to fall to the ground. He could feel the intense heat from the fireball as it passed overhead before crashing into the forest, destroying everything in its path and setting the dry, withering trees ablaze.

"Whoa!" he cried as he tentatively looked up to see more blazing asteroids hurtling down at breakneck speed, about to devastate their target and cause chaos on the earth. Charles picked himself up and ran back down the steps. As he closed the door behind him he heard another fireball hit the ground with a mighty crash which shook the whole mountain. Lisa was waiting for him just inside the entrance.

"Wow, that was close!" Charles exclaimed, still feeling the heat from the heavenly missile.

"It sounds like World War Three out there!" Lisa cried, "I'm going to get the boys to safety!"

"I'll meet you near the deep caves! But I have to go and get our journals from Ezra's room!" replied Charles.

"Are you crazy!?" retorted Lisa.

"Apparently so!" shouted Charles, smiling, as he ran toward Ezra's room.

Charles stepped inside the door of the room when another fireball made a direct hit to the cave. The room shook so violently that books and objects fell off their shelves. Again, Charles found himself on the floor. He staggered to his feet, pulled open the drawer of the desk and grabbed the two journals. He shoved them in his belt and turned around to run for the door, he couldn't believe what he saw; the fire had gone out! The flame that had burned for the entire time they had been there, had been snuffed out! God had left the building!

"Yahweh!" He cried at the top of his voice as another fireball hit the mountain nearby. It was time to leave. He ran down the corridor towards the caves.

Bang! Another one hit, followed by another which shook the whole place. Small rocks began to fall from the roof of the cavern.

"How can this happen?" thought Charles as he ran for cover. "This is the Ark!" He put his hand on the wall to steady himself and felt a violent vibration. A huge crack appeared in the floor where he was standing; the place was collapsing!

It was utter mayhem, with people running everywhere, trying to get cover.

"Head for the caves!" screamed Charles, as he ran towards the tunnels, his hands shielding his head from falling debris. All Charles could think about was Lisa and the boys; he had to get to them. He ran to the furthest part of the caves shouting for people to follow him as he went. Hundreds of people were with him as he rounded what he knew to be the final bend of the tunnel. All that was up ahead was a dead end.

"Lisa!" he called out in desperation, "Where are you?!" Out of the darkness, he heard a shout,

"Charles! We're here!" He went into the dead-end passage and there was Lisa, Jenny, Sophie, the boys and the twins all huddled together taking cover. They all hugged.

"We have to get out of here!" cried Charles, "The Ark is collapsing but this is a dead end!" Lisa recalled the visions and the teaching they had received and knew they had to trust.

"Charles, remember when we were with Ezra and saw Eden!" she shouted over the noise of crashing rocks all around them, "The tunnel carried on! Remember?!"

"But wasn't that in another realm!" shouted Charles in reply.

"Maybe, but we have to trust Yahweh! We can't go back that's for certain and there is no way that we have come all this way to get buried here like this!" She looked all around her and noticed a small corridor leading off the passageway.

"Come on, let's go!" She took hold of Josh and Luke's hands and Charles carried the twins as they ran further into the narrow tunnel. Lisa cried out to the mass of people following,

"This way!" she called out to everyone. "It has to be this way!"

More and more explosions could be heard further back as they ran down the tunnel in complete darkness. Charles followed faithfully, wanting to believe she was right but half expecting their expedition to be very short lived. Somehow, the tunnel kept on going but only wide enough for two or three people.

"Doesn't this remind you of something?!" She shouted, to Charles.

"It sure does!" replied Charles amazed the tunnel had even gone as far as it had, "Ezra said it was real!"

There was a long line of people stretching back, following them down the passageway, desperate to get to safety. The tunnel had become so dark that they couldn't see anything in front or to the side of them, just as before when Ezra led them to Eden. The crashing continued above and behind them as they ran deeper and deeper into the mountain.

"I've been down here so many times and this tunnel is definitely not here!" exclaimed Charles. They laughed together, trusting in the Father.

Lisa whispered under her breath as she ran,

"For you are Yahweh, my God. The Holy One of Israel, my Saviour!" She felt an empowering; a strength from within and a confidence that only comes from Yahweh.

"Faith! Complete Faith!" Lisa cried out. She could sense lots people behind her but could not see them or anything else for that matter.

More and more fireballs could be heard hitting the mountain, causing the ground to shake beneath their feet and rocks to fall from the tunnel roof.

"Come on! Keep going!" Lisa shouted as they headed deeper down the corridor and into the dense darkness.

"Yahweh! Yahweh! Save us!" Lisa shouted, as another falling rock came close. The twins were constantly mumbling something in what sounded like Hebrew as they ran.

Others around her started shouting,

"Yahweh! Hosanna! Save us!" Soon it became a battle cry as everyone ran through the chaos, miraculously dodging falling rocks in the complete darkness that surrounded them. They were heading into the unknown; running on adrenaline and faith, running for their lives and letting The Spirit of Yahweh guide them. They continued to cry out,

"Yahweh! Hosanna! Save us!"

It felt like this tunnel was endless, but they kept running, through the fear; defeating the flesh; knowing that Father God was truly with them. Surely, He would save them! Surely, He would see them through this darkness! Charles could feel his heart pounding; a mixture of excitement, adrenaline and lack of fitness all rolled into one.

Eventually, a tiny light could be seen in the far distance. It hit their eyes like a needle, penetrating the darkness.

"Do you see that Charles?" Lisa cried. He replied emphatically,

"I do Lisa!"

There was a cheer from the group behind them as they all saw the tiny pin prick of light. Somewhere behind them, they could hear Tony Franks 'whooping' for joy like a gibbon and hundreds of others crying out to God in praise. They ran faster as the light got closer and slowly, bit by bit they began to be able to see one other.

"Where do you think this will come out?" Lisa asked Charles, again remembering the times with Ezra.

"I have absolutely no idea!" replied Charles laughing, gasping for breath, knowing that things never happen how you expect them to with Yahweh, "It could be Eden, it could be Monhampton, it could be Heaven! Only God knows!"

It was lovely to be able to see faces again as they drew ever nearer to the light. After checking her immediate family, she turned around to see faces everywhere, stretching right back into the darkness.

"Praise Yahweh, He's brought us through again!" She said thankfully, putting her arms around her boys. Cheers and echoes of Amen and Praises to God could be continually heard way back into the darkness. A waft of air hit their faces as they approached the end of the tunnel along with a huge sense of relief and victory that they had escaped.

They reached the mouth of the tunnel and stepped out into the daylight. They recognised immediately where they were. They were on the far side of the estate, near to the fields they had ploughed with their angelic friends. Although they knew where they were, it looked nothing like the beautiful landscape that they remembered.

"This certainly isn't Heaven!" Lisa cried catching her breath after their run in the dark. She looked around at what used to be such a fantastic sight. She stood with her hands on her hips looking out towards the sea in dismay. Everything looked sad, as far as the eye could see. The Sun and the Moon were still standing side by side, but the sky somehow looked in pain. There was a strange crimson glow across the heavens with small spindly black clouds randomly dotted about and an eerie stillness that caused Lisa to shudder. It looked toxic; without beauty. Man was destroying everything that Yahweh had made so wonderful. The trees were bare, and the grass was brown. It was a sorrowful sight.

"I'm so sorry, Father!" she said shaking her head, "That people could do this to your wonderful creation!"

People flooded out of the tunnel, excited at first and then silent at the sight that met their eyes. As they stood, gazing across the desolate land they could see what appeared to be shooting stars which quickly developed into a celestial firework display. Everyone looked up, enjoying the spectacle but Charles had seen this before. It was more meteors from the belt of Orion burning up as they reached the Earth's atmosphere.

"Take cover!" Charles shouted, "It isn't over yet! Get ready for round two!" Without warning, a huge fireball flew overhead towards the sea followed by another one crashing into what was left of the forest down in the valley. They all crouched down as the thunder ball hit the ground, causing a vast shaking.

Another inferno started immediately in the forest as though dry trees had been soaked in oil. In the sky, they could see more and more fireballs were making their devastating way to Earth. Something catastrophic was about to take place; the end was surely upon them. Many began to wonder why they had been driven out from the safety of the caves only to be exposed to the deadly event taking place around them.

Lisa cried out,

"I will say of YAHWEH, "*He is* my refuge and my fortress; My God, in Him I will trust. Surely, He shall deliver you from the snare of the fowler *And* from the perilous pestilence. He shall cover you with His feathers,
And under His wings you shall take refuge!

Suddenly, Sam shouted from nearby,

"Hey! Come and look at this!"

They turned to where his voice came from and saw him standing alongside a stone structure of some kind. They scrambled over a pile of rocks to get to him. Amongst the rocks stood Sam leaning on a large old stone doorway with a huge closed wooden door. It was the only thing left standing. There were no walls or any other remains; just the doorway. It was a mystery how it was even able to stand.

They gathered around the door. It had an inscription beautifully carved into the stone surround. It read:

Yahshua – Salvation of Yah

I am the door. If anyone enters by Me,

he will be saved.

Lisa ran her hand over the stone and the carved inscription. She turned to the people around her watching;

"Has anyone ever been up here and seen this before?" she asked. No-one had; they just shook their heads. She looked at all the faces in front of her, trying to look for an answer to the questions in her mind. She turned to the door again. It was a huge beautifully made, solid piece of oak that had no handle and no key hole. It was dusty and old but looked unused.

"We have to go through this door! Please don't ask me why! I know we can walk around it, but we have to go through it" she said as she gave it a push. It wouldn't open. Charles and Ben stood either side of her as everyone crowded around. She turned again and looked at Ben for some inspiration. She thought he should have known, after all he was able to interpret all those dreams.

"I really don't know, Lisa!" he said. She looked at him thoughtfully and then turned back to the door without a reply. There was nothing around the sides, only the door post and the back of the door. As she stared at the door she could hear many people coughing behind her with the polluted air.

Another fireball hit the mountain close to them and made everyone crouch to the floor. It was time to pray and not to 'lean on her own understanding'. Yahweh had obviously put this door here, so He would show her the way. She lifted her head to the heavens, held her arms high and cried,

"The house was not the Ark! The caves were not the Ark! But I know you have a safe place for us!" Another fireball whistled overhead, causing everyone to involuntarily duck down.

Lisa cried out again,

"Help us, Abba! Help us!"

She shouted out in prayer amidst the chaos going on all around as more fireballs flew overhead, crashing into a nearby group of trees, igniting them instantly. It looked like the whole world was burning. Rain began to lash down and flashes of lightening lit up the skies as she cried out,

"Yahshua, You are Yahweh, the salvation of Yahweh, You were there in the beginning with the Father! You are God! All things came into existence through You! In You there is life! You are the light of mankind and the darkness cannot hide You! Hosanna! Save us Yahshua! You are the Gate! And whoever enters through You will be saved!

As the 'Amen' echoed out across the valleys there was a loud 'clunk' and the door in front of her slowly started to open by itself. People began to rise to their feet as a bright white light seeped through the opening of the door. As it opened wider, the light flooded over them all, drawing them in, filling them with a feeling of complete peace; in complete contrast to the violent place that they were standing in.

The door opened fully and stopped. Lisa took her boys by the hand and began to walk through with them followed by Sophie, the twins and all of the people. There were many hundreds of them that had made it, they were passing through the door leaving behind a devastated world and entering a new, safe but completely unknown one. Charles stood back and waited for everyone to walk through.

As the last people went through he joined the end of the line and was just about to go through the door himself when he heard a familiar voice shouting him from behind.

"Wait! Charles, wait! Keep the door open for me!"

He recognised it immediately as that of Christopher Adams.

"Of all people!" cried Charles, shouting across the field towards the waving Pastor running towards him,

"What are you doing here?!" The desperate man shouted back against the noise of more fireballs crashing to earth,

"I was wrong! I'm so sorry! Please keep the door open for me!"

Charles walked through the door, knowing that it wasn't his decision and that Yahweh would leave them open for him if he was meant to be in there with them. It closed behind him just as Adams arrived at them. The pastor stood outside banging on the old wooden door; shouting at God,

"Let me in!" he screamed, "God let me in!

I am Your servant!

I prophesied, healed and saw miracles in Your Name!"

The door remained shut.

Chapter Eighteen

Through the door

Everything was bright white; dazzling and yet still comfortable on the eyes. Lisa looked at her boys and the twins who were just in front of her, venturing forward. Light was all around, completely surrounding them; the absolute opposite of being in that pitch-black tunnel. No-one knew where they were but wherever it was, it felt good. There was a feeling of complete serenity, of relief and absolute security, again, so unlike the landscape they had just come from.

The air was very warm and yet beautifully fresh which was so wonderful after being 'cooped up' underground for as long as they had been. Lisa took a deep breath and filled her lungs. She smiled in contentment, realising that they were now in that safe place, having left behind the tribulations of the world. She stopped and turned around; hearing hubby's voice, calling her from behind.

"Hey, wait!" said Charles slightly out of breath after running to catch up with his family, "You would never guess who came running up to the door?!" He answered his own question before Lisa could even attempt an answer, "Christopher Adams!" he exclaimed.

"Wow!" exclaimed Lisa, "He must have seen the error of his ways!"

"Maybe he did." replied Charles, "But the door closed before he could get through!" The parable of the wise and foolish virgins came to Lisa's mind and how sad it felt that someone they knew, even with his faults, hadn't made it. A sense of missed opportunity washed over her; could she have done more?

As they carried on walking, they noticed the light becoming less intense and a landscape started to appear. Soon they found themselves standing in the normal light of day. The group stopped to take in the vista that lay ahead of them; one of open countryside and of hills and valleys. The grass was green but slightly sunburned and the sky was a deep blue with not a trace of a cloud. It was a beautiful sight but wherever they were, it definitely was not Wales; it was far too warm and dry. Lisa put her arms around her precious boys as they gazed across the landscape. She said to them in a calm, soft voice,

"That was quite a scary experience back there, wasn't it?"

"It was awesome!" They replied, completely unnerved with the whole thing, "Totally awesome!"

This place that Yahweh had brought them to, was very real and of this earth, unlike Eden and the vision from the future, but at the same time felt supernaturally special.

The temperature was a lot warmer than they had been used to in Wales and there was a glorious light breeze. Wherever they were was completely idyllic. They could hear the beautiful sounds of birds and the babbling of a stream of water nearby.

"Let's go and have a little rest before we carry on," Charles suggested, "and maybe we can figure out where we are and which direction we should be heading in!"

"Nice idea, Mr Michaels!" Lisa replied, "But how can we know which direction we should be heading in if we don't know where it is we're going!" They laughed. Charles continued,

"But at least we're safe and not having to dodge bombs anymore!"

Everyone followed Lisa and Charles as they wandered down to the nearby stream, where they were able to get refreshed by the beautiful pure crystal-clear water and pick juicy red apples from the trees in the nearby spinney. It was so good to bite into an apple after living on leaves for so long.

"Wow, I've missed fruit!" Lisa remarked wiping the juice from her chin.

"Oh yes, me too!" replied Charles as he and the boys chomped on the delicious apples.

Lisa sat and pondered as she ate. She looked back over the time she had spent with God and all the things that had happened to her and her family. It seemed five minutes ago that she was sitting in her lounge at her house in Hightown reading her bible, watching her boys play with their Lego blocks. Then there was The Ark; Oh, that place! How she loved that old house and the estate! Then of course the greatest time ever with Yahshua! Wow, was that special! Then the disasters struck, and life had been one trial after another until now where she finally felt safe even though she didn't know where she was. Then she had the added bonus of Judah and Ephraim and what a blessing they were. These were truly incredible days they were living in. She thought about the visions; the teaching she had been receiving from Yahweh. Never before had she placed such trust in anything or anyone but now was the time that she needed to do just that for their salvation and survival. She also knew that others needed to gain that trust in Yahweh too. Over the time, she had come to the understanding that the phrase that had started it all;

'You are far more powerful than you have been led to believe', meant so much more than she had first realised. She now understood that her sole purpose in life was to do the will of God and that anything else, as Solomon had so eloquently put it, was meaningless. The power lay in her obedience to Him and that obedience led to life and 'rest for her soul'.

"Hey Mum!" came a little voice behind her, pulling her away from her thoughts. It was Judah with Ephraim. They hugged their Mummy as she sat finishing her apple.

"You are such dear little boys!" she said giving them a squeeze, "Or maybe not so little now!" She giggled with them.

"Mummy?" said Ephraim, "We need to take over guiding you through this land now and lead you all to your destination!" Lisa looked at him with a frown, questioning his statement.

"Why?! Do you know where we are supposed to be going?!" she asked.

"Well, yes of course!" said Judah, "This is why we came here!" Ephraim continued, "To lead you where He needs you to be!"

It was one thing to trust in Yahweh but another to trust and follow two three-week-old children, who had appeared from nowhere and then supernaturally grown and continued to grow by the day. But she also knew how Father God operated and this was just like Him. He always seemed to do things how you would least expect them to happen and this was no different.

"Okay," she said with a warm smile, "I trust you both.... lead on!"

Charles, Lisa, their family and the entire assembly got up from their time of respite and followed Judah and Ephraim through the land, heading off in an easterly direction.

As they walked along, Lisa looked at the twins from behind. Every time they turned around, they seemed to speak out something prophetic. They seemed to grow older and wiser and more filled with the Holy Spirit with every step they took and every decision they made. Again, she thought to herself about the joy that these boys had bought to her life after losing their baby. It seemed so surreal that it was only weeks ago that they came into their lives and now they were guiding them on a journey, fulfilling everyone's destiny.

Charles leaned over and whispered in Lisa's ear,

"So, do you have any idea where we are heading?"

"None whatsoever!" she laughed, "But the twins assure me that they do! Why don't you ask them?!"

"I will!" replied Charles and shouted to their two little guides,

"Ephraim? Judah? Can we ask you a question?" They stopped in their tracks and turned to their Dad. The caravan ground to a halt and everyone gathered around. Ephraim spoke out in his confident voice of authority,
"We will answer anything we are able to! If anyone has questions, let them ask!" Charles was the first to speak up.

"Well yes!" he said, "Do you know where we are?" Judah smiled and said,

"We do!" There was a silence as Charles and everyone waited; expecting him to explain further. All they could hear was crickets chirping and a lark singing high up above them. Judah just smiled. Ephraim asked, looking around the people,
"Anything else?!"

Charles continued,

"So, can you tell us where we are, or is that a secret?"

"Yes, we can and no it's not!" Ephraim replied. Then silence again. Charles looked at Lisa. She looked back and laughed again. She continued,

"I don't think it's for us to know right now, Charles. We just need to trust and follow." Judah smiled, turned and continued to walk; Ephraim frowned and followed suit. The throng followed on, trudging through the beautiful countryside.

"It's not far now!" said Judah, looking ahead as he walked, his brother by his side.

"What isn't?" asked Charles with a degree of frustration. His question was again met with silence; they just walked.

The terrain was becoming more and more rugged as the twins led them through the valleys. The weather was heating up and although it was still pleasant it was necessary to rest now and again.

Ahead, they could see a group of palm trees which Judah and Ephraim made a beeline for and as they got closer they could see that it was a watering hole, to which the twins went straight to and got down on their knees and started to drink from. Everyone followed them and refreshed themselves after the days walk.

The twins sat together on a low wall that surrounded the pool and stretched their legs out. Judah said to the group that was around him,

"This is a well that was dug by your forefather Israel or Yacob as he was then known. Then it was repaired and tended to by the Israelites when they were here with brother Moses." More gathered around them as they continued to speak.

"So, are we in Israel?" Lisa asked inquisitively.

"No, Mum!" replied Ephraim quite definitely and said no more. Judah continued,

"We are at the appointed place, entering into the appointed time that most of history has looked forward to since Adam and Eve ate of the forbidden fruit." Everyone stared intently at the twins who by now took on the appearance of young teenagers.

"We have a short walk ahead and then all will be revealed to you all." Judah smiled, and Ephraim continued firmly,

"Just trust in Yahweh with all your hearts! We are not being elusive, it's just that if we tell you too much your minds will try and figure out everything that is happening and that is not possible for you to do! We would rather confirm to you what your spirit tells you!"

He smiled a rare smile which was lovely to see. Lisa smiled back in return. He continued,

"Just remember, you are totally safe now, in fact you have been ever since you walked down those steps into the caves! You are being protected by the Most High and His angels. Before the Sun goes down all will be made clear to you." Then they looked at each other and said in unison,

"This is our destiny!"

As they carried on walking, Charles looked up into the sky as he said that and noticed that the Sun was alone in the sky for the first time since the earthquake. Curiosity always seemed to get the better of Charles and he couldn't help blurting out,

"So what country are we in?" The twins smiled at each other and stood up, moved through the people before them and continued on their walk. Everyone else got to their feet and followed. Lisa gave Charles a playful dig in the ribs. She said,

"Even though they said all that, you just had to ask, didn't you?!" Charles smiled back at her and replied,

"Well I thought I may just catch them off guard!" Lisa shoved Charles again and they giggled together like two teenagers. It was so comforting and consoling to know that they were being guided and led by their maker and that all that was happening that day had been planned since the beginning of time.

Even though the two boys, who were walking directly in front of them, leading them all through this land wherever it was, were obviously not normally children, they felt to Lisa like they were her own; like she had raised them for ten or so years and not the matter of weeks that it had really been. She knew now that nothing had been left to chance; even their names were significant, and it wasn't an accident that one of them had been clutching a piece of the bible in his hand.

They walked up a small hill and the twins stopped and admired the view ahead of them. They stood at the top of the slope in awe as they gazed across a huge dry, plain shimmering in the heat in front of them. Both Judah and Ephraim held their arms aloft and cried out,

"Praise be to Yahweh, the Most High! We are here!" Everyone gathered around them.

"Welcome to 'Har Mo'ged'!" they shouted.

They turned to the plain with their arms still lifted high and let out a cheer of celebration. Everyone followed suit and cheered along with them, not totally understanding why.

"Where did he say?" whispered Charles.

"I've no idea!" She replied, "It sounded Hebrew to me!"

They carried on walking; a little faster now with a spring in their steps as their destination was obviously very close. The plain in front of them was many miles across but they could just make out mountains on the other side, which were in directly in line with their path if they didn't deviate from it.

The twins were singing songs in Hebrew as they fairly skipped across the dry smooth plain. It was covered in a short sturdy grass that was very easy to walk on, which looked like carpeting as far as the eye could see.

Trying her best to keep up with her sons, Lisa asked them,

"Judah? Ephraim? What did you say this place was called?"

"The mountain that you see directly ahead of us is called, Har Mo'ged, the Mount of the Appointed Time!" Judah said jubilantly pointing with his finger.

"Har Mo'ged?" Charles said to Lisa in a pseudo Hebrew accent, "That sounds like...."

The twins interrupted in unison.

"Armageddon?"

Chapter Nineteen

The Holy Mountain

"So, this is the plain of Armageddon?!" Lisa responded in amazement.

"It is! That's the place! Just spelled and pronounced incorrectly!" Ephraim replied. Lisa questioned them again,

"But you said that we weren't in Israel?!"

"We're not!" Judah replied. Lisa looked at Charles, completely confused.

"Mum," Ephraim continued, making Lisa feel so proud hearing him call her 'Mum', "Many people have got confused as to the whereabouts of 'Armageddon', as they have come to call it and have it mixed up with a town in Israel called 'Megiddo' but that wouldn't make sense! It's the Mountain of the Appointed Times! It's Har Mo'ged! It's...." He briefly paused, and Judah joined him in giving the answer,

".... Mount Sinai!" Lisa and Charles looked at each other again in amazement.

"We're in Egypt!?" Charles blurted out. The twins stopped in their tracks.

"Dad!" complained Ephraim, making Charles feel exactly how Lisa did when he called her 'Mum', even though he was being corrected, ".... Your geography!"

Judah carried on explaining,

"We are approaching Mount Sinai, which is in modern day Arabia!"

"Arabia?!" replied Charles looking amazed as did most of those around them who were listening to the conversation. Judah continued,

"Yes, Arabia! Your ancestors crossed the red sea that Father parted for them, from Egypt into what is now Arabia! Charles interrupted again,

"Ancestors? You say, 'Our Ancestors'?"

Ephraim replied,

"Of course! You are an Israelite! Native born! Don't you know?" Judah and Ephraim looked around at the blank faces before them. They said in unison,

"Yahweh said through Zechariah the prophet,

"I will strengthen Judah and save the tribes of Joseph." "Often referred to as Ephraim," the namesake interjected,

"I will restore them because I have compassion on them. They will be as though I had not rejected them, for I am Yahweh their God and I will answer them. The Ephraimites will become like warriors, and their hearts will be glad as with wine. Their children will see it and be joyful; their hearts will rejoice in Yahweh. I will signal for them and gather them in.
Surely, I will redeem them; they will be as numerous as before.
Though I scatter them among the peoples, yet in distant lands they will remember me.

They and their children will survive, and they will return."

…. And here you are!"

"I am an Israelite!" stated Charles, "How cool is that!"

"You are indeed!" answered Judah, "As are all of you! Some native born, others grafted in! But still Israel! That is, of course, why you are here! It's because of Yahshua that you can be here!"

They looked around at the people again, who seemed puzzled that they could not have known that they were now part of Israel. Judah carried on,

"The native-born Israelites are made up of twelve tribes but today only the Jews are recognised as Israelites. This is because most of Judah have kept their identity and know who they are to this day. The rest of Israel, the Ephraimites...," Judah paused and slyly glanced over at his brother then continued, ".... were divorced and cast off by Yahweh because of their adulteries. Over time they lost all knowledge of who they were; all trace of their identity was gone. It was the greatest of tragedies." They both hung their heads, muttering something in Hebrew under their breath. Ephraim continued,

"They mingled in with the gentile nations, fulfilling all that Yahweh had spoken, even beginning to worship the gods of the gentile nations. They cast aside the culture of Yahweh's kingdom and adopted the cultures and traditions of the nations and their false gods. They were truly lost. The heavens wept when it seemed the Father's children had gone too far and forgot their heritage." Judah took over,

"Yet He promised to redeem them! But how could this happen? After all, His own word says that a woman cannot return to her husband once he has divorced her and He will never go against His own word!"

Ephraim interjected,

"Whatever He says, He does!

Judah continued,

"But our eternal Father had a master plan; a mysterious and beautiful story; the greatest love story ever to be told; as Paul the Benjamite calls it.... the profound mystery!" He paused and looked around at the faces before him; engrossed in their words. He continued,

"He himself, would come in the form of Man, born of a virgin and give His own life in place of His beloved. Through Yahshua, the adultery of Israel was washed away. He took upon Himself all of her sin; her lawlessness. He paid the price of the death penalty so that she could be released from her guilt and consequential punishment. His blood was shed, so His bride could be made pure and the way was opened for her to return to her first love. It's because of Yahshua's death that you can be saved! And it is because of His resurrection, coming back to life, that He can be the groom!" Judah stopped, holding back tears. Ephraim took over,

"Whether you have Hebrew ancestors like Mum and Dad do or not, you are Israel! If you adorn yourself like a bride, wearing the covenant symbols of a wedding ring, opening your heart to His Spirit, inviting Him to write His perfect Torah on the tablet of your heart, calling His Sabbaths delightful, meeting with Him and all of Heaven at His festivals, the appointed times marked on His calendar; if you do these things, you are Israel! If you partake in His covenant, you are Israel! Just as it says in Ezekiel forty-seven verse twenty-two!" The twins looked around and concluded in unison,

"The Church has NOT replaced Israel....

The Church IS Israel!"

Everyone was silent; teaching like this they had never heard before.

Lisa asked,

"So, if we are Israel, do we belong to a specific tribe? How do we know our lineage?"

"Good question, Mum!" replied Judah, very proud of his mummy, "You will be allotted a tribe at a later date as most of your actual lineage has been lost over the centuries of time."

"Yes!" responded Ephraim, "But your inheritance is still valid and because of your faith in Yahshua, along with obedience in hearing and doing, you have been counted worthy to escape and so, you are here! You have been through purification by trial as others are now going through tribulation in the world." Judah followed on by saying,

"The restoration of Israel is beginning right now and that's all twelve tribes and the foreigner, not just the Jews. I am a Jew because I am of Judah, a Jewish Israelite but Ephraim here," his brother smiled, "He is of Joseph, an Ephraimish Israelite! Is all that clear?"

Lisa laughed,

"I think so! But aren't you both twins?"

Judah continued,

"Yes....but we're a bit different than everyone else!"

Lisa and Charles looked at them in amazement.

"Where did they learn all this?!" whispered Charles in Lisa's ear as not to arouse the attention of the twins.

"In Heaven, I guess." she replied softly.

"That's right Mum!" answered Judah, "In His Kingdom, which is about to come to Earth and His will be done as it is in Heaven."

"Come on! Let's go!" demanded Ephraim, "We have an appointment to keep!"

They set off again walking through the beautiful countryside of Arabia, pondering on all the things that they had just learned from the twins. What lay ahead of them they did not know, but one thing that they had learned was how to walk in faith.

They walked briskly across the arid plain, every step bringing them nearer to that great mountain, which they could now clearly see in the distance; the hallowed place that they had read about all their lives.

As they were approached the middle of the plain, Charles spotted movement over to his left, way ahead of them.

"Look!" he cried, "People!"   They looked across the vast plain to what looked like another great line of people heading towards the mountain.

"Over there too!" shouted Sam, pointing to the right.

"And there!" Shouted someone from the rear. It seemed that there were others who had been on the same mission as they had, and they had all timed it perfectly to arrive at the same time.

The lines of people began to converge as they got closer and closer to the mountain and they could see the other people much clearer and could even make out some of the details of their faces. Everyone looked excited to see each other and some started to wave at other groups. It was amazing to see so many happy people in one place. They felt a unity, a oneness with them; all there for the same reason; a Holy convocation.

This was the body; the bride of Messiah.

At the front of each line there were two younger people leading the way, guiding the people, just like Judah and Ephraim.

"Spooky or what?" said Sam from behind Lisa as they realised the similarity of each of the groups. Many other groups could now be seen too from far left and right. This was indeed a gathering of major proportion. More and more of His faithful were gathering at His Holy Mountain.

Lisa thought to herself,

"I wonder if they all been through what we have? Where are they all from? Did everyone get supernaturally transported over here just as we did?"

Judah and Ephraim signalled some strange hand signal to the small leaders at the front of another line, which looked like something from a sci-fi movie. They, in turn, smiled and signalled back.

They all continued to walk, step by step getting ever closer to their destination; the great mountain of God. Lisa's mind drifted again into times of study that she had spent at the Ark.

"Mount Sinai!" She thought to herself, "The place where the Israelites gathered after escaping from Egypt and being pursued by Pharaoh and his armies; witnessing and walking through the miracle of God at the Red Sea! And now history was repeating itself. They, after going through many trials, had been redeemed and had now been brought to the foot of the very same place!"

She patted her thighs as she walked to make sure this was real and not some kind of vision as she had experienced before. She seemed to be solid enough; the ground seemed hard although a little soft underfoot; she could feel the warmth from the Sun on her face and smell the fresh air of the countryside around her. It had to be real. Again, she thought back to events that had occurred in the past months; all the ups and down, meeting her Messiah, the disasters, the pain, physically and emotionally of losing her baby and the joy of finding the twins, the visions, the police raid followed by more disasters. She knew the difference between real and visionary, natural and supernatural and this was definitely in the naturally real category.

The mountain was now towering over them. It was truly spectacular, not only in its size and grandeur but also because of its prestigious history and the cataclysmic events that had taken place there.

"This is the place where Yahweh met with Moses and gave him His great law and commandments," she thought to herself, "His Torah; the instructions that could lead a man to blessings or curses. This was the very place where Yahweh had proposed to all of Israel and gave her the terms of the marriage covenant, the covenant that Israel had broken causing their tragic scattering. But now here they were, returning to their Husband, this time ready to say "Yes" to being faithful.

Israel had come full circle, fulfilling in perfect detail, thousands of years of prophecy recorded in the scriptures."

The words that the twins had shared earlier made so many things click into place. So many things that once didn't make sense, were now crystal clear. She almost wished that she could have the opportunity to read her bible all over again with this new understanding in mind and that more people could have known these truths.

Suddenly, the twins stopped as did all the other groups. Not a sound could be heard. Everywhere they looked, there were men, women and children. The lines had come together to literally form a sea of people, all standing in silence, wondering but excited about what was coming next. Thousands upon thousands of believers; all gazing upon the wondrous sight that was before and all around them.

Tears were streaming down the faces of many, as the truth began to sink in as to where they were and why they were there. They

215

were at the event that everyone in the world wanted to be at; the time when Yahshua was to return and be with His bride. Amazingly, they had all been counted worthy enough to escape the tribulation that was now upon the earth and were to be a part of the proceedings that would be the beginning of the end of the world as we know it and seeing the Kingdom of Yahweh come to Earth, with King Yahshua reigning supreme.

The silence was broken by the guides, who together let out a shout of Jubilation; they had arrived at the destination and had fulfilled part of their destiny.

People began to mingle and talk with others from different groups, discovering that they were indeed from all over the globe. All had incredible stories to tell of how Yahweh had pulled them out of the disasters and had hidden them in various places of safety.

As they were talking with a couple from the USA, Lisa felt an arm on her shoulder and Charles felt one on his. They turned around. It was Judah and Ephraim. They had now grown into young men; their hair was shoulder length and they both had the beginnings of facial hair.

"Wow! Look at you two!" Lisa exclaimed with pride.

"Two fine young men!" agreed Charles.

"Mum, Dad." Judah began, "We have to go now."

"Go where?!" asked Lisa, concerned about the tone of Judah's voice. Ephraim continued,

"We are going to Jerusalem to give testimony of Yahshua!" They said together,

"It is our destiny!"

A strange emotion of pride and sadness filled Charles and Lisa as they realised what this meant. They both knew that they we not likely to see them again. As hard as it was, Lisa knew that she had to let them go. She kissed them both firmly on the cheek. Charles did the same.

"Thank you so much for being our parents!" said Judah softly.

"Out of all the witnesses, we had the best!" professed Ephraim. Then they turned and walked away.

All the twins, twenty-four in all, grouped together on the plain and held hands in a circle. A whirlwind of dust appeared and encircled them and then disappeared as fast as it came, to leave just two fully mature men standing together. They waved to the assembly and headed off, on their mission to the Holy Land.

Lisa and Charles wrapped their arms around each other as they watched their boys disappear into the distance.

"Wow" said Luke and Josh in unison.

"Do you think we'll ever see them again?" Lisa asked, wiping a tear away with her hand. Charles replied, fighting back the tears,

"I hope we do, sweetheart"

Suddenly, Charles was distracted, noticing some movement on the mountain. He interrupted Lisa, who was trying to explain to the boys, what they had just seen and where their brothers were going. He leant over towards her and whispered in her ear,

"Hey Lisa! Look!"

She turned towards the mountain in the direction of Charles' finger, to see lots of men dressed in white robes coming down towards them. As they got closer to them Lisa recognised one of the men in white.

217

"There's Eli!" she said nudging Charles, "They're angels!"

Eli was obviously heading for their group as his eyes were intently fixed on Charles and Lisa.

"And look who else?" Charles responded. Behind Eli they could make out the familiar faces of Jonah, Joshua and Noah; their four angelic friends. They had a glow about them that was not of this world and an air about them that overflowed with confidence and strength. It was great to see familiar faces in an unfamiliar land.

After the angels had greeted Lisa, Charles and the rest of the group, they stood before them in a line. The other angels did exactly the same before other groups.

Eli began to speak; as he had many times before; without moving his mouth. He spoke directly to everyone as individuals, which was kind of weird; it was like having him on a personal stereo without the earphones.

"Welcome and hello again to you, Lisa." he said, "We are standing right now at the foot of the great Mount Sinai, the Har Mo'ged and you have been brought here by the Most High because of your obedience and willingness to lay down all things of the world and follow His ways, His instructions." Lisa felt overwhelmed and as he spoke, she thought back to all the times that she had made so many mistakes and fallen short in so many ways.

"You are human, Lisa!" Eli responded. Lisa laughed,

"I forgot you can hear my thoughts!" Eli laughed with her, "Yes I sure can, loud and clear!"

"But how did I get here?" she questioned her angelic friend, "I mean after all, I'm no-one! I'm just little old me!"

Eli smiled and replied,

"That's nothing to do with me, Lisa!" She responded,

"Are you sure you haven't pulled any strings!"

Eli explained,

"Lisa, a heart that is set to follow the Lamb wherever He goes, is a heart that pleases Yahweh! Please follow us as we show you the places of history around here and enjoy your reward!"

Lisa looked at Charles and smiled. He had received the same message only addressed to him personally, as had everyone else there.

"How do they do that?" She asked. Charles just shrugged his shoulders, took her by the hand and beckoned to the boys and they followed the angels.

Eli and their other assigned angels proceeded to give them a guided tour. They saw the site where the ancient Israelite camp was set out and where the tent of meeting was built. The events of the past, that made up history, became so real as everything was described to them in great detail by their wonderful angelic guides.

They continued on with their tour and stepped onto the mountain itself and began to ascend. Their first stop was at the rock where Yahweh had passed before Moses. It was hard to process that they were standing at that very place. Eli described all that had happened there and then carried on up the mountain with all following apart from Lisa and Charles, who stayed to admire the spectacle. She put her hands on the rock. She felt a warmth and an energy that travelled up her arms and into her body.

Could the power still be there after all those centuries of time or was she just imagining it?

She closed her eyes. In her mind, she could see the whole event taking place and the conversation between Moses and Yahweh. She placed her cheek on the rock and it tickled her face as she did, a feeling of intense power, yet warm and comforting like waves of love flowed through her body causing her knees to almost buckle.

"Yahweh, Yahweh, compassionate and gracious!" she whispered, "Slow to anger and abounding with love!" Charles touched Lisa's shoulder and the power flowed through him too. He leant on the rock to steady himself and looked directly into Lisa's eyes. She had a glow on her face as though she had been in the presence of Yahweh himself. Charles remarked,

"No wonder Moses' face shone the way it did! But it suits you girl!" They smiled at each other; it was an experience they would never forget.

"We should go!" said Charles standing up straight. Lisa prised herself away from the rock and they all ran to catch up with the group. They knew what was coming next and didn't want to miss out.

As they looked up, they noticed the peak of this marvellous mountain looked darker than the rest of the rocks. It actually looked singed! Burnt by the very fire of God! The tour halted as they reached an area where the ground levelled out and at the edge of the area was a huge flat rock, as big as a house. There were slabs of rock coming away from the mountain; perfectly smooth. Eli explained that this was where Yahweh had made the tablets on which He wrote down His Law for mankind. It was a magical place. Everyone was perfectly quiet and transfixed with the sight that was before them. It was as though their spirits truly connected with what had gone on here all those many years ago. The four angels stood before them all. As usual Eli spoke up.

"This is the place where God met His people!" He cried out, this time his mouth moving. "After Adam and Eve were thrown out of the Garden, this was the first place that Heaven truly met Earth!

This is the place where the power was given back to man; the place where the agreement between the divine and mortal man was laid out; that if man would have followed they would have known a life of Shalom, of peace, safety and total security. The difference between life and death, blessings and curses, everything and nothing!" He paused looking around at the intensity that people stared at him with. He continued,

"You are here seeing this because of your hearts, because of your willingness to put down tradition and find truth. He rewards those who diligently seek Him!"

The angels made a sign with their hands exactly the same as the twins had made and cried out something in 'Angelic', that indescribable guttural sound that left you in no doubt as to who they were. He continued,

"The time draws near for us! A time that all creation has waited for since its birth! Let us go down the mountain and await His presence; the Holy One, our Most High Elohim!" Everyone cheered. Even though they had lived through great miracles and seen great visions at the Ark, it was still hard to take in that all this was really happening.

They all meandered their way back down the mountain, not seeing any of the other groups until they got to the plain before the slopes of the mountain. The excitement and anticipation was thick and electrifying and could be felt, as they mingled with the other groups. It was a vast multitude; many, many thousands of people who were all there because of their obedience and faithfulness and totally committed to pleasing their maker and not man. Unlike the real world, where people were now having to follow the evil one and take the mark or die, they were totally safe and living a life full of the supernatural, just how God designed it to be.

Lisa and Charles looked around at all the people they had come to know and love at the Ark. It was amazing to be sharing in this with them. They could see Sam, the eternal comedian, chatting away with others making them laugh; Jenny and Ben engaged in deep conversation with another couple and her own boys, Josh and Luke confidently talking to two elderly people. This experience had obviously been an indescribable blessing for them all. A feeling of complete peace washed over Lisa as she pondered the many things that had happened since the realisation that she was far more powerful than she had been led to believe and what that truly meant. The events of last few weeks hadn't seemed real and many times she had had to 'pinch' herself, to check that she still wasn't dreaming. What lay ahead, she had no idea but what she did know was that all the people that were close to her were now safe in the hands and will of God.

The angels began to re-gather on the slopes of the mountain. Something was about to happen as an air of expectation descended on them. Even with this, they jumped to attention, as an almighty blast of sound hit them. The sheer volume of noise caused the ground to shake violently, the sound filled the entire skies. It was a powerful sound like a mixture of trumpets and thunder coming from the heavenlies.

This was what mankind had all been waiting for, for many centuries. He was on His way.

Chapter Twenty

Behold He Comes!

Charles, Lisa and the boys all held each other's hands as they were filled with an awesome fear and an excitement like they'd never witnessed before. The blast of the trumpet was so loud that small rocks came rolling down the mountain towards them as the ground shook. It was all consuming. For certain, something spectacular was about to happen.

Lisa squeezed Charles' hand one more time when suddenly there was a white flash, covering the whole sky, that made everyone gasp and stand back in awe. They looked up; their eyes totally fixed on the sky and the view that was before them, as thousands upon thousands of tiny white flickering lights began to descend from the blueness above them. The contrast of the blue sky and the white lights was indescribable; so magnificent, so regal.

More trumpet blasts filled the airwaves and a sound of what was like a vast choir began to rain down on the people below. It was so beautiful and yet powerful and majestic, that no-one could utter a whisper; they were completely awestruck. Lisa stood open mouthed at the immense sight before her eyes. She looked at Charles by her side, who was in exactly the same state, as was everybody else around her.

Angels were singing songs of worship; filling the skies with such wonderful splendour. People began to weep for joy at the glorious sight before them. As the white lights descended on them, they could see that they were, in fact, more angels dressed in pure white. They bore two sets of white wings, one larger pair at their shoulders and a smaller pair from their lower back. Many hovered above them, blowing trumpets and singing, as more and more heavenly beings poured out of the sky.

Without notice, there was another huge flash, that spread across the entire sky, followed by a clap of thunder that again shook the ground. The Trumpets all blew together and the angels all cried out together:

"Holy, Holy, Holy!"

With their eyes fixed on the skies, a light brighter than the Sun began to come down towards them, surrounded by thousands upon thousands of angels. Those that were around them blew their trumpets with abandon and the choir sang with increasing intensity. They could see the bright light getting nearer and in the centre of the light was the figure of the King of Kings, Yahshua, their Messiah. As He got nearer, everyone, angels and humans alike, cried out to Him once again,

"Holy, Holy, Holy!"

Instantly, everyone's clothes were replaced with white robes and golden rope sashes around their waists, that shone brightly with the reflection from the great brightness above them. Lisa looked at Charles for a second, in pure joy, thinking how handsome he looked in his robes and how proud she was of this man, before looking up again.

As He got close to them, two angels took His arms and lowered Him slowly to the ground and then, there He was, standing before them on the mountain. They were all awestruck at the wondrous sight before their eyes. His appearance was so majestic. Light drenched the whole area as He turned His head from side to side, smiling approvingly, slowly gazing across the sea of faces before Him.

He held his arms out and everyone bowed their heads and fell to their knees. The mountainside was covered by a thick blanket of angels all bowing before him in the same manner. He stood there in all His splendour. His robe glistening in the light as though it was encrusted with tiny gems. He wore a golden sash around His waist which matched the golden strip around the edges of His robe. His hair was as bright as snow on a sunny day and His eyes shone with an intensity that pierced through them as though He were able to see right into the hearts of His people before Him. He opened His mouth and began to speak to the multitude; everyone lifted their heads as He said,

"Look at my Bride! Look how beautiful you are!"

He spoke to each person listening to Him as though He was addressing them personally. Lisa, Charles and everyone hearing His voice, loved Him deeply. They all smiled and cheered as He spoke.

"Come!" He said and beckoned them to Him. He turned and walked up the mountain. The multitude flooded onto the slopes of the foothills of the sacred mountain, following their Messiah the bridegroom.

Yahshua stood before them all as the crowd gathered before Him.

"My beautiful bride!" He said with a beaming radiant smile,

"I have known you for so long and watched over you. I have waited for this moment, when we could come together like this.

You have followed me and held tight to my Father's instructions, even when it cost some of you your lives; you have adorned yourself as a bride and made yourselves ready. I stood here

225

once before; I gave the marriage covenant to my people, your forefathers, Israel. I gave her the same gospel that you were given, I gave her my instructions and My Sabbaths.

I promised to be a husband to her, to love her and cause all of my goodness to be poured over her, but she was stubborn and faithless. She quickly broke my covenant and strayed far from the ancient path. But You, my love, you returned! You received the gospel and combined it with faith. You embraced my Torah and with childlike faith, you obeyed. You allowed me to wash you with my word. You sought me with all of your heart and you found me. You recognised my voice and you followed. Through tests and trials, you remained obedient, when the shepherds tried to lead you from the narrow path you remained unmoved. You were rejected by men and betrayed, even by those you thought belonged to me. I saw your troubles, I felt your pain, when you lost those you loved for the sake of holding onto my truth. I treasured your tears and brought them before my Father when I prayed for you; how I have prayed for you! Now, here you stand, before me, you have returned with you whole heart, you have been found worthy to escape the hour of trial and to be called my bride."

As Yahshua spoke, Lisa felt a love that words could not begin to fully describe, the feeling poured over her like warm summer rain. Overwhelmed by His mercy and grace, she began to weep tears of pure joy.

The bride began to celebrate.

Lisa and Charles looked around at all the wonderful people. It had been an incredible journey for them all.

Lisa was just about to say something when she felt someone standing beside her. It was Yahshua. They fell to their knees in the presence of their Saviour.

"Get up Lisa, Charles! Come sit with me!"

They got to their feet and Lisa flung her arms around His neck.

"I've missed you too!" He said laughing.

They all sat down and Yahshua kissed Lisa's hand. He kissed Charles on the cheek and looked them both in their eyes. It was amazing to see the robe that He was wearing up close. It had fine encrusted diamonds woven into the material that shone with a radiance that could only be made in Heaven. Yahshua said in a voice filled with compassion,

"I know the love you have for those people who haven't made it to this special time. This is a time reserved for my bride; those who have worn the symbols of our marriage covenant. Don't worry, those who have not made it here will have another chance! They will be invited to the great wedding celebration as guests, but first they must be purified! People have been warned for thousands of years to be ready, for faith without works is dead!"

He gripped their hands and the arms of His robe rode up a little to reveal His scars once more to them. He continued,

"I taught my people that they must purify themselves so that they could escape tribulation, but their lack of belief in my word left them unprepared, without the oil of my Torah. A tear rolled down His precious face as He continued,

"I love them dearly, Lisa, Charles. Whether they have made it now or later has no bearing on my love for my people. For their sake, I will soon bring an end to the troubles that are now taking place."

Yahshua smiled and said while getting to His feet,

"Oh, there is so much to do Lisa! Our journey together has only just begun!" He smiled again with His charismatic smile and

227

squeezed their hands. "Why don't you go and explore this wonderful place." He continued, "I think you'll like it! We have lots of time to really get to know each other." He kissed Lisa's hand and Charles' cheek again and winked at Luke and Josh, who were sat opposite and as quickly as He appeared, He disappeared.

Charles looked at Lisa and said,

"Wow! How amazing is His love! He is so incredible!" Lisa said nothing. She was so overwhelmed by everything. She just wiped the tears from her face and smiled. Charles hugged her. "Let's do as Yahshua suggested and let's go and explore!" he said standing to his feet. The boys jumped up too.

"Yay! Let's go!" they cried, tugging at their mums' arm, pulling her to her feet.

"Okay, okay!" she relented, and they headed off down the mountain. As they turned by the rock where Yahweh had shown himself to Moses, they could see the plain beneath them at the foot of the mountain.

"Someone has been very busy while we've been up here!" Charles remarked.

"Wow! That's amazing!" replied Lisa.

"Cooool!" responded Josh and Luke and they all hurried down towards the gentle slopes of the foothills, to the city that had been created for them. There was line after line of white tents, all beautifully laid out, each one equidistant to the other. There were, what seemed like, thousands of them laid out in four groups, surrounding a larger tent in the middle. It was exactly how they had seen the drawings of the camp of the Israelites in teaching books on the very subject. The large tent in the middle was of course the Tent of Meeting where God had given Moses the model of the Temple. It looked a lot larger, grander and more ornate than they had imagined. It was a truly beautiful sight.

As they approached the camp there stood an angel with a scroll in his hands. They walked up to him and Charles was just going to say who they were when the angel beat him to it and said just two words,

"Joseph, seven." Then he handed them a small sealed scroll and pointed them in a direction.

Each of the paths between the tents were named after one of the twelve sons of Jacob; the tribes of Israel and it didn't take them long to locate 'Joseph'. The numbers descended towards the centre of the camp and the boys ran ahead shouting out the numbers of each tent to their Mum and Dad. Other people were wandering around trying to locate their tents as the Michaels family marched down 'Joseph', Charles clutching the scroll in his hand.

"What do you think the scroll is all about?" Lisa asked not able to hold in the question for a second longer.

"I've no idea as always!" replied Charles laughing, "But let's find our accommodation first!"

"Oh you!" laughed Lisa, "How are you able to be so patient!"

They hurriedly walked in search of number seven, with Josh and Luke skipping ahead of them still shouting out numbers. They got right down to the front and shouted,

"Here it is!" They jumped for joy as Mum and Dad followed behind them. They were indeed on the front row, with nothing more than the huge Tent of Meeting before them.

"Wow! That's impressive!" whispered Charles in a quiet, voice.

"It certainly is!" replied Lisa, standing by his side looking at this incredibly ornate canvas structure before them.

"Mum! Dad!" the boys shouted, pulling their attention away from the temple, "Our tent! Our tent!" Charles pulled the front tent flap to one side and they all went in to cries of "Wow!" and "Awesome!" It was a tent the likes of which they had never seen before. Although fairly plain white on the outside, it was completely different inside. They all stood for a while in the centre of the tent which was surrounded with individual rooms for them all. There were beautiful silk cushions all around for them to sit on and the floor was covered with some kind of material which was like a thick piled carpet without the pile, but as soft, deep and comfortable. The ceiling was draped in veils and decorated with vines bearing fruit. Other exotic plants adorned the room, all with fruit on their welcoming branches. The boys soon picked their rooms and Mum and Dad's. There were giant cushions to sleep on and more veils draped across the ceilings. It was an amazing luxurious palace even though it was still a tent.

They were all laughing and shouting for joy when a familiar voice came from the doorway,

"So, you like it then?" It was Yahshua again. They all ran to Him and hugged him.

"This is amazing!" cried Lisa.

"All for you my bride!" replied Yahshua, "All for you!"

They hugged all the more. He continued, "We will all stay here until the next appointed season. You are safe here!" He looked at Charles and said,

"Do you have the scroll, Charles?"

"Yes, I do!" Charles replied and handed it to Yahshua.

"No, no!" He replied, "It's for you to open!"

Charles looked at the scroll and broke the seal. He unrolled it and read,

"To Charles, Lisa, Luke and Joshua: YOU are far more POWERFUL than you have been led to BELIEVE!"

In an instant, memories flooded back to all the occasions when they had seen this message and now here they were here with Yahshua in a tent at Mount Sinai reading the same thing. Tears of joy and relief streamed down their faces.

Yahshua took them by the hands and they stood in a circle, all five of them. He bowed His head and they prayed to the Father,

"My dear Abba, thank you for this family! Please anoint them now!" Lisa, Charles, Josh and Luke all fell to their knees and Yahshua stood over them. He said proudly,

"There, my bride!" He touched their foreheads with His hand.

"You carry the Name of my Father and myself.

You are sealed!"

Chapter Twenty-One

Time Cut Short

The days that followed were magical; a time that people throughout the centuries could have only dreamt of. Every one of the thousands of people at the mountain got to spend time alone with Yahshua to look back over the past and to talk of the future; their destiny and how the decisions they had made had brought them to this place.

The trials and tribulations of the outside world were rarely talked about, but angels travelled back and forth, reporting to Yahshua of the calamities and the atrocities that were taking place. Many people were being deceived by a false messiah who had set up a tent of meeting in Jerusalem. The ark of the covenant had been found and this false messiah demanded that all worship before the ark. The people who had realized that this was not the true messiah and refused to worship him, were being tortured and killed. The role of reporting all this during this time seemed to be very important and they always got the attention of Messiah. Although He devoted His time to the bride, He never forgot those who were going through tribulation and persecution. Troubled and desperately concerned for them He wept as He prayed to the Father that they would hold out and not give in to the ways of the world.

Many times, He could be heard repeating His words to Matthew all those years ago,

"Do not be afraid of those who kill the body but cannot kill the soul. Rather, be afraid of the One who can destroy both soul and body in hell."

"Even if they are killed," He told Lisa and family one day, "they are blessed, for they have been persecuted for My sake and they will see the Kingdom of Heaven. They just need to hold on!"

Every Sabbath, everyone gathered at the foot of the mountain and listened to Yahshua, who would hold everyone totally captivated with His words. He never needed to make an explanation of anything He said, as everything made complete sense. So much from the past, that Lisa had been confused about, now was as clear as crystal to her.

She loved Yahshua with every fibre of her being; a love that was so natural, as a child has for its mother. It was so different to her love for Charles; it was a complete infinite love; one of total security and safety. Likewise, His love for her was so strong, that He had died for her and she knew that He would have done so, if she had been the only person left in the world.

He was a champion to all in every way; even to those who weren't with them, who were going through such terrible times and had no idea of what was to come. He died so that all those who were lost in a wicked and sinful world could be redeemed and brought back to the safe place and once again be married to Him.

When He spoke, His words had a depth and an authority like no other words she had ever heard. They came out of His mouth and took immediate root in her heart. Lisa still felt that she had so much to learn and yet, here she was at the Mountain of the Appointed Times with the Creator of all things.

As the months were rolling on, it was becoming increasingly obvious that another significant event was drawing near. The troubles of the world had the attention of the whole company of Heaven and yet they were all still living the 'dream'. There was a deep sense of security at Sinai; of shalom, that totally overshadowed any thoughts between the people, of the inevitable war ahead. Yahshua never became unnerved but there were times when clearly the angel's feathers were being ruffled. More and more reports were flooding in from angels concerning the troubles with the saints and the trials they were being subject to.

One day, out of the blue, as Yahshua was conversing with angels, He spoke out; loud enough for everyone there to here. He cried,

"Enough! We go to war!"

His words echoed around the whole plain of Sinai and everyone automatically turned their eyes to their Messiah. He stood on the mountain, before the whole assembly, completely surrounded by angels of many different shapes and sizes. He commanded,

"We need to go now, or no-one will survive!"

The angels all turned and went separate ways all except one giant angel with long flowing black hair and a huge shiny sword which was the length of his body. He bore scales of some sort, like armour. He had two large powerful wings and four smaller ones; two at the bottom of his back and two at his neck; a magnificent looking creature, obviously made for warfare. He stayed a few minutes and left with purposeful intent, his eyes like stone, looking at no-one. Yahshua turned to the crowds and addressed everyone.

"My dear bride! Our time here was meant to be much longer, but we must cut our celebrations short for the sake of my people. All men need to report to your allotted angels and prepare yourselves for war! Orders have been sent out and our angels will now allow the allies of the enemy to gather and surround us here. Prepare yourselves for battle! Prepare yourselves for victory!" There was a great cheer. As it died down He continued,

"We will surely prevail and draw the days of the enemy to a close. He must be defeated and locked away for one thousand years!"

Lisa looked at Charles who was so excited about the words he had just heard and the forthcoming battle ahead. He punched the air with his fist. He turned to Lisa,

"Who would have ever believed, that I get to fight in the battle of Armageddon!?" he exclaimed with tremendous pride. Lisa was not so excited, although she smiled at Charles in his glory, not wanting to steal his thunder. She loved his company and the love that they shared and although she knew his loyalty was of course to Yahshua, she secretly hoped that he could have a different task than being on the front-line battling with the warriors.

Sam and Ben came over to Charles and 'high-fived' with him, just to cement his enthusiasm.

"Can you believe it!?" He said, grabbing a shoulder of each of his two great friends, "We get to be part of the most famous battle of all time.... Har Mo'ged, Armageddon!"

Josh and Luke came running up to Lisa, pulling her focus away from her husband's excitement.

"Mummy, do you think we'll get to fight!?" Josh enquired hopefully.

"Not a chance!" replied Lisa emphatically. She thought to herself. "What was it with men, that they all seemed to love a good fight?" All she wanted was for this to be over and enjoy their lives together with Yahshua. She hugged them both, stroking their hair as she did. Their wanting to be involved with the men made her smile and gave her a warm feeling of pride but at the same time her motherly instinct naturally wanted to protect them. She looked at them with love and compassion and said softly,

"You will both have something much more important to do than fight!" They hung their heads in disappointment. "Those who are behind the scenes are just as important!" Lisa consoled them, looking into their eyes. "Remember what Yahshua said about those who will have other things to do?" They nodded in response. "Well, that's where you fit in.... wars aren't won on the battlefield alone." They grinned at each other and walked away to find Sophie, proud in the belief that they would have a role to play in the victory against satan.

The hours ahead were like a scene from a Hollywood epic. The horses where being groomed and equipped for battle. The angels handed out symbols for the horse's battle dress depicting which tribe the men belonged to.

Sam was given his symbol and came running over to Lisa, like a child, to show it to her. It had a unicorn on it.

"I'm with the tribe of Ephraim!" he said proudly with a huge smile on his face.

"And I'm Judah!" exclaimed Ben, lifting his symbol for Lisa to see. "Look at this Lion!"

"Very nice!" Lisa replied, "What has Charles been given?"

"I've no idea!" responded Sam, "In fact I haven't seen him for a while."

The sudden sharp sound of a trumpet blew and made everyone turn and look towards the direction it came from. The huge warring angel with the long, flowing black hair was standing on a rock alongside an angel in white with the ram's horn. The whole assembly went quiet and the big man-like creation prepared to speak.

"The mouth of Yahweh has spoken!" he began. The angels cheered in response. He continued,

236

"The gates have been opened and the enemy has been summoned and has begun to gather! It is time.... at last! As we speak we can see the dust that they stir; the hatred that they have for anything good, anything of the Almighty! So, let's gird our loins and fight for our King and we shall have victory! I, Michael, leader of the army of Yahweh, know the tactics of the enemy and how hard they will fight, but remember.... you are chosen, you are sealed! We shall have victory!"

There was a great cheer from the whole congregation, angels and humans alike and Michael stood down and was followed by his entourage of warriors.

Lisa looked around for Charles. He was normally, never far away but she hadn't seen him for some time now. No sooner had she started to get concerned, when she heard a voice behind her.

"We have to go to the tent, Lisa." It was Charles. He had a very serious, downcast look on his face, one that Lisa had never seen before in the time that she had known him. She replied cheerfully,

"Okay, let's go!" He remained sullen. "Is everything alright?" she asked.

"Not really!" he grumbled with a sad expression. They started to walk towards their tent. He continued, "I have no symbol!"

"Oh really?! That's strange?!" Lisa questioned.

"It means I'm not fighting!" said a disappointed, Charles. Lisa stopped in her tracks and grabbed Charles by the arm. She appeared troubled but deep down she felt an immense sense of relief lift from her body.

"Why?" she questioned, trying to look concerned for his sake.

"I have no idea, that's why we are going to the tent, I guess, to find out." He paused, then continued, "I mean.... Sam is fighting, Ben is, John is.... everyone is.... all except me!" Lisa took his hand and tried to console his disappointment.

"Well, they must have something really important for you to do, Charles; something way more important than fighting!" She said giving his hand an extra squeeze as they approached the tent. "After all, anyone can fight!"

Charles pulled the door flap to one side and let Lisa through. He followed her in and immediately they both fell to the floor at the sight that met their eyes. Their two boys, Josh and Luke were lying prostrate on the rugs alongside their adopted sister Sophie, at the feet of Yahshua. He stood before them tall and strong, glowing in a way that He must have done on the Mount of Transfiguration in the bible. His white robe shone brightly as though He was outside in the glorious sunshine. He wore a sash of gold around his waist and a white cloak over his shoulders which was red all around the bottom as though it had been dipped in blood. He had a long, shiny sword at his side on which they could see four Hebrew letters engraved;

Tav, Vav, Reysh, Hey.

Lisa knew this translated to mean 'Torah' or 'Instructions' in English. On His head, He wore a crown which sparkled with huge gemstones and smaller diadems within pure almost translucent gold nestling in the long white locks of His hair.

As awesome and powerful as He looked, from His mouth came words in a loving and caring manner.

"Get up, my children." He said, "I need to talk to you about something." They all got up onto their knees and knelt before Him.

"Many times, I have heard you question, "Just what is the Ark? Is it the home of Mr Carter? Is it the underground cavern?" Most believe the Ark is the Ark of the Covenant that carried precious artefacts and the commandments of the Father. The Spirit dwelt there, and the power was the presence of Yahweh. Right now, I choose the ones who love me with all their heart, soul and strength and carry my laws deep in their hearts! They have kept hold of the Father's truths and rejected the words of man." Lisa nodded in agreement. He continued,

"So, what is the Ark?" He paused for a second and smiled that wonderful smile and said,

"The Ark that you have been searching for is not a place!"

He paused again, waiting for a reaction but instead they all just stared inquisitively. He continued,

"Remember when you both searched for the definition of an Ark in the dictionary?"

"You were there?!" Lisa blurted out and immediately realised how silly her reaction was. She thought, "Of course He was there!" She quickly and apologetically corrected herself. She stuttered,

"I mean, sorry, yes of course You were there!" Yahshua laughed,

"Yes, I was there!" He continued, "I've always been there! Apart from the Ark which carried Moses to safety and the one that protected Noah and creation from the flood, there were two definitions of an Ark that you read about and they are correct! But there is more!" He paused once again, as they all waited with 'baited-breath,

"Firstly, it is a place of refuge, of safety and protection….

I am The Ark! Through your obedience to The Word, following in My footsteps by walking in The Fathers instructions, you will enter into the Ark!" He smiled and continued,

"Secondly, the Ark is a vessel, a container that carries the Commandments of God and by His Spirit, those Commandments are written on hearts rather than just tablets of stone. So, Lisa, Charles, Sophie, children...." He smiled again; they could feel pure love pouring from Him.

"…. You are the Ark!...

…. Those who 'Keep the Commandments of God and hold to My Testimony'!" He looked into the eyes of those before Him, searching every thought.

"And last but by no means least....

…. The Ark is a parable!

…. It is the account of everything that you have seen, and it is to be written before it all takes place."
Lisa thought to herself, not wanting to interrupt again, with a slightly worried look on her face,

"All of this has to be written down?! Wait! Our journals! Oh, my goodness! That's why we made so many notes! But, isn't it too late now?! I mean, we are here aren't we? Is this real or has it all been a dream?!"
Yahshua replied, knowing her every thought,

"Oh yes it's real, Lisa…." He laughed, stepped forward and took hold of Lisa's hand. He lifted her to her feet and put one hand on her waist and held her other hand at shoulder height in a dance position. He looked her in the eyes and said,

"…. But it is yet to happen!" He moved forward and led her in a dance, turning her around and around, His hair and robe flowing as He did. Lisa laughed for joy. She still hadn't fully understood what

Yahshua meant but she wanted to enjoy this precious moment. Charles stood up and cheered and applauded his Saviour and sweetheart doing a turn around the floor of the tent; the boys and Sophie joining in, laughing and loving every second of this magical time with their King. Then He stopped and they all sat down again and Yahshua finished His sentence, looking at them intently.

"All that you have seen must soon take place and all that you have experienced will certainly happen, but first it is to be written!" There was a small silence.

He looked at the slightly confused, but happy expressions of the family before him. He explained further,

"The parable is a call to my Bride to make herself ready, to fan the dying flame in the hearts of those who have become weary and wounded by the storms and trials of life."

Lisa nodded, and a tear rolled down her cheek as she remembered how she had felt in the past. Yahshua continued,

"Some will read the words of the parable and know that I am speaking to them." He took Charles and Lisa by the hand and lifted them both to their feet and looked into their eyes. The beauty of His eyes was breath-taking, filled with intense compassion and love. He said softly,

"Lisa, Charles, I desire for *all* of my people to be safe with Me when the time of great trouble is upon the whole earth. It is at hand, but many are not ready. They have fallen from the narrow path, led astray by the doctrines of men; some into the error of lawlessness! Some believe that I came to set aside the precepts of my Father's eternal covenant. Others, who once loved me as their God and King have lost their faith in Me and who I am. Others, still are broken and weary and have stopped their good works because of unbelief. Then, there are those who have become discouraged! They have faced fierce battles and have walked through a great time of loss, betrayal and sorrow. The visions which I placed within them, appear to have been crushed into dust under the weight of life's storms. I want you to

241

remind them that gold is refined only through intense heat! If they allow their trials and even tribulation to refine them, they may be found worthy to escape this time of trouble that we are seeing now!"

He continued "Tell them that the path which leads to life is narrow, it's an uphill climb and is full of challenges! But this is *My* Path and if they continue on it they will find Me, waiting for them with their reward."

When Yahshua spoke the words 'it's an uphill climb', Lisa immediately had a flash back to the night her and Charles woke to see the twins prophesying, the words which seemed like a riddle at the time now made perfect sense.

Yahshua continued, "The parable will remind them of my love and show them the way back to the ancient paths, where I am to be found."

There was silence as everyone sat listening with awe as Yahshua spoke of how the battles we face, are the very things that refine us and prepare us to be His Spotless Bride. Lisa finally understood why James had written, 'that we should count it pure joy when we face all kinds of trials.' Lisa thought to herself,

"Trials are exactly what Yahweh uses to refine and perfect us!" Yahshua replied,

"Blessed are the poor in spirit, for theirs is the kingdom of heaven.

Blessed are those who mourn, for they shall be comforted.

Blessed are the meek, for they shall inherit the earth.

Blessed are those who hunger and thirst for righteousness, for they shall be satisfied.

Blessed are the merciful, for they shall receive mercy.

Blessed are the pure in heart, for they shall see God.

Blessed are the peacemakers, for they shall be called sons of God.

242

Blessed are those who are persecuted for righteousness' sake, for theirs is the kingdom of heaven.

Blessed are you when others revile you and persecute you and utter all kinds of evil against you falsely on my account. Rejoice and be glad, for your reward is great in heaven, for so they persecuted the prophets who were before you."

There was another long silence as Yahshua's words seemed to penetrate their souls. The words which they had read in Matthew five many times were now more alive than ever before.

As they listened to Yahshua, Charles and Lisa experienced the same mix of emotions at the very same moment; elated that they finally understood things which had never fully grasped before, but deeply grieved as they pondered how many people had never come to know these truths and wondered if there was more that they should have done to at least try and share these treasures with more people.

Charles gasped as a realization hit him;

"That evening!" He said, "The evening I said to Lisa that we should write a book sometime.... and call it The Ark.... was that a prompt from You!?"

"It was, Charles, it was! There have been many occasions when I have spoken to you and you thought it was your own voice!" Yahshua laughed and hugged Charles. "Remember that I am with you always! I will never leave your side!" He stepped away from him and moved towards the door of the tent.

Yahshua beckoned to the family and said,

"Follow me!"

They had read those words, 'Follow me!' in the gospels many times and it was amazing to hear it themselves, from His very mouth.

They followed and Yahshua held the door open for them. As they passed Him to go through He whispered to them,

"See, I have placed before you an open door that no one can shut!"

The tent door flapped in the wind and in the blink of an eye Yahshua had gone and they found themselves back in the tunnel under the mountain in Wales. They were immediately greeted by their old friend, Ezra.

"Come this way!" He said to them and led the way down the corridor towards what they knew was the main cavern of the ark. They were all completely bewildered, gobsmacked and yet said nothing; they just followed, knowing that they were totally in God's hands.

They arrived at Ezra's old room and he held the door for them and they all stepped inside. It was just how they remembered it the very first time they found it; the fire was burning again with its eternal flame. The chair was in front of the fire, just as it was when they first met him and over the back of the chair, draped his old prayer shawl. Ezra picked up the shawl from the chair and put it over his shoulders. He turned around and backed slowly towards the chair to sit down. As he sat down on the creaky chair, his face turned old again and his body became haggered and bent over. His face, now lined with tears, just how he was when they first met. He looked up to them and said, "Now go! Call out to the children of the Most High. Show them the way back to the ancient path!"

"Ezra," said Lisa, "I don't understand!" But before she could say anything else, Ezra was back in the state that they found him, weeping and not responding to anybody.

Charles took Lisa's hand and said to her, Sophie and the boys,

"Come on, let's go figure out what's going on!"

They made their way to the large old door at the entrance, which led to the steps to outside. Charles opened the door and they followed him up the steps. When they got to the top of the steps they found that instead of being outside, they were in a room. They were in the old house! Everyone gasped but no one could speak. The house looked just as it did when they first came to see it, before any cleaning or decorating had been done!

Suddenly, they heard voices coming from the direction of the living room. They all looked at one another and without a word walked in the direction of the voices. They walked into the living room to find Jenny sitting with Old Mr Carter.

"Jenny!" shouted Josh. There was no reaction or response from either of them.

"Mr Carter!?" said Lisa inquisitively, but still no response. They obviously couldn't see or hear them. The boys waved wildly in front of Jenny, but she didn't flinch.

"So, Jenny, have we had any enquiries yet?" asked Mr Carter.

Jenny replied, "Nothing yet, Mr Carter, but I have sent an advert to the local newspaper, which will start running next month."

"Well," said Mr Carter, "everything is ready now and Yahweh has given me many dreams, showing me the person, He has chosen to carry the baton from here. I know it must be soon because He has also shown me that I have completed my work."

"Charles, why can't they hear us? asked Lisa, "What is going on?" Charles was about to try and produce some sort of explanation, which would bring some reassurance but as he opened his mouth to speak, a loud thud was heard coming from outside. They all rushed toward the front door. Charles went first, holding his arms slightly outward, to protect his family from whatever they may face outside. He opened the door cautiously and stuck his head outside. The coast was clear. Nothing untoward and no obvious cause for the loud thud. He stepped outside and began to make his way around the deck. Wanting to reassure his family a little, he said,

"I don't know how to explain all of this right now, but I do know that minutes ago, we were all with our King, who gave us a task. Maybe we need to forget figuring this out and start doing what He said!" When he got no reply, he turned around hoping for a response. Everyone had disappeared. "what is going on" Charles cried.

245

He was alone. He ran back toward the front door, but it was locked.

"Lisa!" he shouted, while knocking on the door. "Sophie, Luke, Josh!"

A heavy hand rested on his shoulder causing him to jump and turn around. "Eli! Where is Lisa?!" he cried.

Eli replied, "Charles, remember what you heard…. Yahshua said that all you have seen must now take place, it has not happened yet!"

Charles struggled to process Eli's words and responded "Eli, are you telling me that it was all a dream? None of it was real? Please, tell me that Lisa is real and that I'm not in love with an imaginary woman!?

"Charles, Lisa is real, it was all real, it just hasn't happened yet! You were shown what is about to happen and now you must go find her, find Lisa! But before you go, here, you're going to need this!"

Eli reached out his arm and in his hand was a small white business card. Charles took it from him and looked at it.

It had his name on it….

'Charles Michaels'

He turned it over and written in pen were the words….

'You are far more powerful than you have been led to believe.'

Chapter Twenty-Two
When The End Meets The Beginning

It was hard for Lisa to concentrate. The kids, happy to be home after a long day at school, had just tipped out the bucket of building blocks and were thrilled at the noise it had made, screaming at each other as they scattered the blocks to flatten the pile. The TV was blaring with an action cartoon, as an alien life form had captured the hero, holding him to ransom to try and steal from him the key to the universe.

"I'm trying to read, boys!" Lisa complained, but as usual when they were in full flow, they totally ignored her request to calm down and carried on with their high-volume banter. She shuffled in her chair, sitting more upright, her head bowed down staring at the book on her lap and continued to read with an even more intense focus, trying to battle through all the noise and distraction. She found herself staring at the same passage in her bible, over and over again. The words seemed to jump out from the page; almost separating themselves from the rest of the passage, drawing her in. It was as though she couldn't read past those few lines. The more she looked at them, the more they seemed to radiate, almost pulsating in front of her eyes.

The passage was from the book of Matthew, where Jesus was talking with the rich young man about entering the kingdom of heaven. It read, 'Jesus looked at them and said, "With man this is impossible but with God all things are possible!"'

The context of the passage didn't seem to matter, it was just the line itself. It was just those particular words of Jesus', "...but with God, all things are possible!"

She repeated them under her breath, only her lips moving as she soaked up the words of her Saviour. She started to day dream.

She suddenly found herself back in her childhood, listening to her teacher in primary school, ranting on at her in front of the whole class: "If you carry on like that, Lisa, you'll never amount to anything! You're useless!" The teacher's stern voice echoed around in her head over and over again along with the merciless laughter of her so-called classmates. She felt the trauma, embarrassment and humiliation of the whole episode as though she was right back there in that dimly lit, dingy classroom.

The classroom transformed into the kitchen of the house she grew up in and she was standing there, as a teenager in front of her parents having a finger wagged in her face, being told by her father, "You're just a thorn in my side! Why didn't we get a son instead of you?" She felt the pain, hurt and frustration of those times, all those years ago, as though she was reliving it right there and then.

The face of her father evolved into the accusing, angry grimace of her drunken husband, bellowing at her as a young adult. She could smell the beer on his breath as he shouted into her face, "Why can't you look like her?" he screamed as he forcefully prodded and pointed at a glamour model on the overturned page of a men's magazine. "Why did I get stuck with you?"

Again, the feeling of inadequacy and unworthiness felt as real in her mind as it did at the time. Her heart pounded with anguish as she sat there in her chair, blankly staring at the bible on her knee; the pressure and stress of the pictures in her mind felt like more than just a figment of her imagination. To top it all she could hear the familiar sound of the voice in her own mind confirming what these characters from her past were saying.

"You're a failure!"

"You'll never get out of here!"

Suddenly she woke from the reverie with a start as the alien on the TV screamed at the hero, who was bound to a pillar. "You are not as powerful as you have been led to believe! Just give in!"

The alien's words seemed to reverberate around in her head. She looked down at her bible on her lap.

"With God all things are possible."

Then she looked back at the TV as the alien continued to attempt to intimidate his captive, knowing that if he could just make the hero doubt himself, he could overpower him.

She felt as though a revelation was unfolding before her very eyes, that with God she could do way more with her life, more than she had ever thought possible! Could it be that she had been held back from realising her own potential? Could it be that she, just like the hero, had been made to doubt her own abilities and had all those negative instances in her life been an attempt to keep her from becoming the person she was meant to be? Could it really be that to God she was significant and capable of achieving so much more - that He had a genuine plan for her; a calling on her life?

The End?

About the Author

Since writing *the Ark,* Ian left the beautiful country of Wales to spend a year in Southern Spain, with his family to work for Revelation TV alongside Lisa as prayer co-ordinators. Ian, Lisa and their two sons Ian jr. and Oliver have now returned to the UK. They are currently establishing a vison which they have carried in their hearts for many years to launch a Christian Publishing operation to produce their own titles and help and to provide a platform for the works of other Christian writers. You can keep yourself up to date with current and future titles by visiting their Facebook page https://www.facebook.com/ianjervisauthor

Printed in Poland
by Amazon Fulfillment
Poland Sp. z o.o., Wrocław

61836046R00145